Contemporary Stories

Selected and edited by
Nick Jones

Oxford University Press

Oxford University Press, Walton Street, Oxford OX2 6DP

Oxford New York Toronto
Delhi Bombay Calcutta Madras Karachi
Petaling Jaya Singapore Hong Kong Tokyo
Nairobi Dar es Salaam Cape Town
Melbourne Auckland

and associated companies in
Berlin Ibadan

Oxford is a trade mark of Oxford University Press

© Selection and Notes: Nick Jones 1986

Fifth impression 1991

ISBN 0 19 831251 2

Cover: *Figure Composition No. 1 (1944–45)* by Edward Burra.
Reproduced by permission of Alex Reid and Leferre Ltd, London

Set by Oxford Publishing Services, Oxford
Printed and bound in Great Britain at
the University Press, Cambridge

Contents

Acknowledgements

The editor and publishers wish to thank the following for permission to reprint copyright material:

Chinua Achebe: 'Civil Peace' from *Girls at War*. Reprinted by permission of Heinemann Educational Books.

J G Ballard: 'The Drowned Giant' from *The Terminal Beach* (Victor Gollancz Ltd.). Reprinted by permission of Margaret Hanbury.

George Mackay Brown: 'Gold Dust' from *Andrina*. Reprinted by permission of the author and The Hogarth Press.

Raymond Carver: 'Bicycles, muscles, cigarets' from *Will You Please Be Quiet, Please?*. Reprinted by permission of the author and Collins Publishers.

Anita Desai: 'Games at Twilight' from *Games at Twilight*. Reprinted by permission of William Heinemann Ltd.

Farrukh Dhondy: 'KBW' from *East End at Your Feet* (Macmillan). Reprinted by permission of the author and David Higham Associates Ltd.

Nadine Gordimer: 'Town and Country Lovers' from *A Soldier's Embrace*. Reprinted by permission of Jonathan Cape Ltd.

Penelope Lively: 'Next term we'll mash you' from *Nothing Missing but the Samovar*. Reprinted by permission of William Heinemann Ltd.

Bernard Mac Laverty: 'The Exercise' *from Secrets and Other Stories* (Blackstaff/Allison and Busby). Reprinted by permission of the author and Blackstaff Press Ltd.

Gabriel Garcia Marquez: 'The Handsomest Drowned Man in the World' from *Leaf Storm*, translated by Gregory Rabassa. Reprinted by permission of Jonathan Cape Ltd.

Alice Munro: 'Red Dress 1946' from *Dance of the Happy Shades* (Allen Lane). Reprinted by permission of Penguin Books.

Joyce Carol Oates: 'The Giant Woman' from *Nightside* (Victor Gollanez Ltd). Reprinted by permission of the author, and Murray Pollinger.

William Trevor: 'Broken Homes' from *Lovers of Their Time* (The Bodley Head). Reprinted by permission of A.D. Peters and Co. Ltd.

Alice Walker: 'Nineteen Fifty Five' from *You Can't Keep a Good Woman Down* (Women's Press). Reprinted by permission of David Higham Associates Ltd.

Preface

This collection of stories aims to engage the feelings and the imaginations of young adult readers, and to offer some sense of the range of contemporary fiction available to them.

The fourteen stories are 'contemporary' in that all were published within the last twenty years – and most within the last ten – by authors who are still very much alive and writing. Some of the names are likely to be new to the English classroom, but each has already made a substantial contribution to the body of contemporary fiction, and the 'Commentary' recommends other suitable titles by the writers concerned.

Apart from Gabriel Garcia Marquez, the authors included write habitually in English, and may certainly be considered part of 'English Literature' in the school sense, though curiously not one of the fourteen authors was actually born in England. This diversity of origin is a reminder of the vigorously international nature of the English language in the contemporary period, and one likely source, I would hope, of the book's attraction.

The section at the back contains a page or so of open-ended commentary on each of the pieces included, which aims to encourage a wide-ranging discussion of the stories among those who read them. There are also ideas for written work arising out of such discussion. Some are essay titles of a traditional kind; others suggest a more oblique approach, exploring creatively some facet of the subject matter of the story, or using some aspect of the writing as a model for the production of original imaginative work. It is certainly my hope that the book will be read as much in the context of writing stories as of writing essays – though neither activity need take precedence over the enjoyment and appreciation of the stories themselves.

To claim that the selection is 'representative' of the contemporary short story in English would be misleading: it remains the partial and restricted choice of an individual reader, conscious of the limitations under which such a book is likely to be used. I have nonetheless attempted to balance the choice of stories in a number of ways, and hope that it may therefore serve as a random sampler, at least, of the richness and diversity of contemporary fiction in English. If readers of this anthology go on to make a habit of reading books by these authors and others like them, then its purpose will have been amply served.

Nick Jones

Games at Twilight

Anita Desai

It was still too hot to play outdoors. They had had their tea, they had been washed and had their hair brushed, and after the long day of confinement in the house that was not cool but at least a protection from the sun, the children strained to get out. Their faces were red and bloated with the effort, but their mother would not open the door, everything was still curtained and shuttered in a way that stifled the children, made them feel that their lungs were stuffed with cotton wool and their noses with dust and if they didn't burst out into the light and see the sun and feel the air, they would choke.

'Please, ma, please,' they begged. 'We'll play in the veranda and porch – we won't go a step out of the porch.'

'You will, I know you will, and then—'

'No – we won't, we won't,' they wailed so horrendously that she actually let down the bolt of the front door so that they burst out like seeds from a crackling, over-ripe pod into the veranda, with such wild, maniacal yells that she retreated to her bath and the shower of talcum powder and the fresh sari that were to help her face the summer evening.

They faced the afternoon. It was too hot. Too bright. The white walls of the veranda glared stridently in the sun. The bougainvillea hung about it, purple and magenta, in livid balloons. The garden outside was like a tray made of beaten brass, flattened out on the red gravel and the stony soil in all shades of metal – aluminium, tin, copper and brass. No life stirred at this arid time of day – the birds still drooped, like dead fruit, in the papery tents of the trees; some squirrels lay limp on the wet earth under the garden tap. The outdoor dog lay stretched as if dead on the veranda mat, his paws and ears and tail all reaching out like dying travellers in search of water. He rolled his eyes at the children – two white marbles rolling in the purple sockets, begging for sympathy – and attempted to lift his tail in a wag but could not. It only twitched and lay still.

Then, perhaps roused by the shrieks of the children, a band of parrots suddenly fell out of the eucalyptus tree, tumbled frantically in the still, sizzling air, then sorted themselves out into battle formation and streaked away across the white sky.

The children, too, felt released. They too began tumbling, shoving, pushing against each other, frantic to start. Start what? Start their business. The business of the children's day which is – play.

'Let's play hide-and-seek.'

'Who'll be It?'

'You be It.'

'Why should I? You be—'

'You're the eldest—'

'That doesn't mean—'

The shoves became harder. Some kicked out. The motherly Mira intervened. She pulled the boys roughly apart. There was a tearing sound of cloth but it was lost in the heavy panting and angry grumbling and no one paid attention to the small sleeve hanging loosely off a shoulder.

'Make a circle, make a circle!' she shouted, firmly pulling and pushing till a kind of vague circle was formed. 'Now clap!' she roared and, clapping, they all chanted in melancholy unison: 'Dip, dip, dip – my blue ship—' and every now and then one or the other saw he was safe by the way his hands fell at the crucial moment – palm on palm, or back of hand on palm – and dropped out of the circle with a yell and a jump of relief and jubilation.

Raghu was It. He started to protest, to cry 'You cheated – Mira cheated – Anu cheated—' but it was too late, the others had all already streaked away. There was no one to hear when he called out, 'Only in the veranda – the porch – Ma said – Ma *said* to stay in the porch!' No one had stopped to listen, all he saw were their brown legs flashing through the dusty shrubs, scrambling up brick walls, leaping over compost heaps and hedges, and then the porch stood empty in the purple shade of the bougainvillea and the garden was as empty as before; even the limp squirrels had whisked away, leaving everything gleaming, brassy and bare.

Only small Manu suddenly reappeared, as if he had dropped out of an invisible cloud or from a bird's claws, and stood for a moment in the centre of the yellow lawn, chewing his finger and near to tears as he heard Raghu shouting, with his head pressed against the veranda wall, 'Eighty-three, eighty-five, eighty-nine, ninety . . .' and then made off in a panic, half of him wanting to fly north, the other half counselling south. Raghu turned just in time to see the flash of his white shorts and the uncertain skittering of his red sandals, and charged after him with such a blood-curdling yell that Manu stumbled over the hosepipe, fell into its rubber coils and lay there weeping, 'I won't be It – you have to find them all – all – All!'

'I know I have to, idiot,' Raghu said, superciliously kicking him with his toe. 'You're dead,' he said with satisfaction, licking the beads of perspiration off his upper lip, and then stalked off in search of worthier prey, whistling spiritedly so that the hiders should hear and tremble.

Ravi heard the whistling and picked his nose in a panic, trying to find comfort by burrowing the finger deep-deep into that soft tunnel. He felt himself too exposed, sitting on an upturned flower pot behind the garage. Where could he burrow? He could run around the garage if he heard Raghu come – around and around and around – but he hadn't much faith in his short legs when matched against Raghu's long, hefty, hairy footballer legs. Ravi had a frightening glimpse of them as Raghu combed the hedge of crotons and hibiscus, trampling delicate ferns underfoot as he did so. Ravi looked about him desperately, swallowing a small ball of snot in his fear.

The garage was locked with a great heavy lock to which the driver had the key in his room, hanging from a nail on the wall under his work-shirt. Ravi had peeped in and seen him still sprawling on his string-cot in his vest and striped underpants, the hair on his chest and the hair in his nose shaking with the vibrations of his phlegm-obstructed snores. Ravi had wished he were tall enough, big enough to reach the key on the nail, but it was impossible, beyond his reach for years to come. He had sidled away and sat dejectedly on the flower pot. That at least was cut to his own size.

But next to the garage was another shed with a big green door. Also locked. No one even knew who had the key to the lock. That shed wasn't opened more than once a year when Ma turned out all the old broken bits of furniture and rolls of matting and leaking buckets, and the white ant hills were broken and swept away and Flit sprayed into the spider webs and rat holes so that the whole operation was like the looting of a poor, ruined and conquered city. The green leaves of the door sagged. They were nearly off their rusty hinges. The hinges were large and made a small gap between the door and the walls – only large enough for rats, dogs and, possibly, Ravi to slip through.

Ravi had never cared to enter such a dark and depressing mortuary of defunct household goods seething with such unspeakable and alarming animal life but, as Raghu's whistling grew angrier and sharper and his crashing and storming in the hedge wilder, Ravi suddenly slipped off the flower pot and through the crack and was gone. He chuckled aloud with astonishment at his own temerity so that Raghu came out of the hedge, stood silent with his hands on his hips, listening, and finally shouted 'I heard you! I'm coming! *Got* you—' and came charging round the garage only to find the upturned flower pot, the yellow dust, the crawling of white ants in a mud-hill against the closed shed door – nothing. Snarling, he bent to pick up a stick and went off, whacking it against the garage and shed walls as if to beat out his prey.

Ravi shook, then shivered with delight, with self-congratulation. Also with fear. It was dark, spooky in the shed. It had a muffled smell, as of graves. Ravi had once got locked into the linen cupboard and sat there weeping for half an hour before he was rescued. But at least that had been a familiar place, and even smelt pleasantly of starch, laundry and, reassuringly, of his mother. But the shed smelt of rats, ant hills, dust and spider webs. Also of less definable, less recognizable horrors. And it was dark. Except for the white-hot cracks along the door, there was no light. The roof was very low. Although Ravi was small, he felt as if he could reach up and touch it with his finger tips. But he didn't stretch. He hunched himself into a ball so as not to bump into anything, touch or feel anything. What might there not be to touch him and feel him as he stood there, trying to see in the dark? Something cold, or slimy – like a snake. Snakes! He leapt up as Raghu whacked the wall with his stick – then, quickly realizing what it was, felt almost relieved to hear Raghu, hear his stick. It made him feel protected.

But Raghu soon moved away. There wasn't a sound once his

footsteps had gone around the garage and disappeared. Ravi stood frozen inside the shed. Then he shivered all over. Something had tickled the back of his neck. It took him a while to pick up the courage to lift his hand and explore. It was an insect – perhaps a spider – exploring *him*. He squashed it and wondered how many more creatures were watching him, waiting to reach out and touch him, the stranger.

There was nothing now. After standing in that position – his hand still on his neck, feeling the wet splodge of the squashed spider gradually dry – for minutes, hours, his legs began to tremble with the effort, the inaction. By now he could see enough in the dark to make out the large solid shapes of old wardrobes, broken buckets and bedsteads piled on top of each other around him. He recognized an old bathtub – patches of enamel glimmered at him and at last he lowered himself onto its edge.

He contemplated slipping out of the shed and into the fray. He wondered if it would not be better to be captured by Raghu and be returned to the milling crowd as long as he could be in the sun, the light, the free spaces of the garden and the familiarity of his brothers, sisters and cousins. It would be evening soon. Their games would become legitimate. The parents would sit out on the lawn on cane basket chairs and watch them as they tore around the garden or gathered in knots to share a loot of mulberries or black, teeth-splitting *jamun* from the garden trees. The gardener would fix the hosepipe to the water tap and water would fall lavishly through the air to the ground, soaking the dry yellow grass and the red gravel and arousing the sweet, the intoxicating scent of water on dry earth – that loveliest scent in the world. Ravi sniffed for a whiff of it. He half-rose from the bathtub, then heard the despairing scream of one of the girls as Raghu bore down upon her. There was the sound of a crash, and of rolling about in the bushes, the shrubs, then screams and accusing sobs of, 'I touched the den—' 'You did not—' 'I did—' 'You liar, you did *not*' and then a fading away and silence again.

Ravi sat back on the harsh edge of the tub, deciding to hold out a bit longer. What fun if they were all found and caught – he alone left unconquered! He had never known that sensation. Nothing more wonderful had ever happened to him than being taken out by an uncle and bought a whole slab of chocolate all to himself, or being flung into the soda-man's pony cart and driven up to the gate by the friendly driver with the red beard and pointed ears. To defeat Raghu – that hirsute, hoarse-voiced football champion – and to be the winner in a circle of older, bigger, luckier children – that would be thrilling beyond imagination. He hugged his knees together and smiled to himself almost shyly at the thought of so much victory, such laurels.

There he sat smiling, knocking his heels against the bathtub, now and then getting up and going to the door to put his ear to the broad crack and listening for sounds of the game, the pursuer and the pursued, and then returning to his seat with the dogged determination of the true winner, a breaker of records, a champion.

It grew darker in the shed as the light at the door grew softer, fuzzier, turned to a kind of crumbling yellow pollen that turned to yellow fur, blue fur, grey fur. Evening. Twilight. The sound of water gushing, falling. The scent of earth receiving water, slaking its thirst in great gulps and releasing that green scent of freshness, coolness. Through the crack Ravi saw the long purple shadows of the shed and the garage lying still across the yard. Beyond that, the white walls of the house. The bougainvillea had lost its lividity, hung in dark bundles that quaked and twittered and seethed with masses of homing sparrows. The lawn was shut off from his view. Could he hear the children's voices? It seemed to him that he could. It seemed to him that he could hear them chanting, singing, laughing. But what about the game? What had happened? Could it be over? How could it when he was still not found?

It then occurred to him that he could have slipped out long ago, dashed across the yard to the veranda and touched the 'den'. It was necessary to do that to win. He had forgotten. He had only remembered the part of hiding and trying to elude the seeker. He had done that so successfully, his success had occupied him so wholly that he had quite forgotten that success had to be clinched by that final dash to victory and the ringing dry of 'Den!'.

With a whimper he burst through the crack, fell on his knees, got up and stumbled on stiff, benumbed legs across the shadowy yard, crying heartily by the time he reached the veranda so that when he flung himself at the white pillar and bawled, 'Den! Den! Den!' his voice broke with rage and pity at the disgrace of it all and he felt himself flooded with tears and misery.

Out on the lawn, the children stopped chanting. They all turned to stare at him in amazement. Their faces were pale and triangular in the dusk. The trees and bushes around them stood inky and sepulchral, spilling long shadows across them. They stared, wondering at his reappearance, his passion, his wild animal howling. Their mother rose from her basket chair and came towards him, worried, annoyed, saying, 'Stop it, stop it, Ravi. Don't be a baby. Have you hurt yourself?' Seeing him attended to, the children went back to clasping their hands and chanting 'The grass is green, the rose is red. . . .'

But Ravi would not let them. He tore himself out of his mother's grasp and pounded across the lawn into their midst, charging at them with his head lowered so that they scattered in surprise. 'I won, I won, I won,' he bawled, shaking his head so that the big tears flew. 'Raghu didn't find me. I won, I won—'

It took them a minute to grasp what he was saying, even who he was. They had quite forgotten him. Raghu had found all the others long ago. There had been a fight about who was to be It next. It had been so fierce that their mother had emerged from her bath and made them change to another game. Then they had played another and another. Broken mulberries from the tree and eaten them. Helped the driver wash the car when their father returned from work. Helped the gardener water the beds till he roared at them and swore he would complain to their parents. The parents had come out, taken up their positions on the cane chairs. They had begun to play again, sing and chant. All this time no one had remembered Ravi. Having disappeared from the scene, he had disappeared from their minds. Clean.

'Don't be a fool,' Raghu said roughly, pushing him aside, and even Mira said, 'Stop howling, Ravi. If you want to play, you can stand at the end of the line,' and she put him there very firmly.

The game proceeded. Two pairs of arms reached up and met in an arc. The children trooped under it again and again in a lugubrious circle, ducking their heads and intoning

'The grass is green,
The rose is red;
Remember me
When I am dead, dead, dead dead . . .'

And the arc of thin arms trembled in the twilight, and the heads were bowed so sadly, and their feet trampled to that melancholy refrain so mournfully, so helplessly, that Ravi could not bear it. He would not follow them, he would not be included in this funereal game. He had wanted victory and triumph – not a funeral. But he had been forgotten, left out and he would not join them now. The ignominy of being forgotten – how could he face it? He felt his heart go heavy and ache inside him unbearably. He lay down full length on the damp grass, crushing his face into it, no longer crying, silenced by a terrible sense of his insignificance.

The Giant Woman

Joyce Carol Oates

'Get away! Get away! Get out of here!'

She came at us, swinging something. It struck the side of the shed – there was a metallic sound – and then her screaming again.

'—out of here—I'll kill—'

The others were ahead of me. I ran, whimpering with fear.

Behind us she stood at the end of the dirt path, screaming. Her words had lost their separate, distinct shapes; they were all one furious uncontrollable sound.

I ran panting and whimpering with fear. The others were in the cornfield – nearly at the creek bank – I could hear them laughing and squealing. I nearly fell, the cornstalks caught and tore at my face, I could hear her still screaming behind me and it was mixed with my own sobbing. I knew she had stopped at the edge of the path, on the hill. I knew she was not chasing me. But I could not control my terror.

At the steep creek bank they had stopped for breath. They were not waiting for me, they had forgotten me, they were gasping, laughing, Donna was doubled over with laughter, Albert was poking and jabbing her; it was all a joke, the whole thing was a joke.

Donna stared at me. 'Look at her, look, the baby's crying. – Hey, don't cry, she isn't going to get you. She isn't going to do anything, she's too old.'

Albert was still laughing.

'Shut up, stop crying,' Donna said.

'I'm not crying—'

'Just be quiet.'

'She was so goddam mad—' Albert said.

They descended the steep hill, sliding down, grabbing at bushes and exposed tree roots. I couldn't go down that way because it was too steep. I went the long way around, on a path the fishermen used, but even so I stepped on loose dry pebbles and fell; I cried out in surprise more than pain, and at the bottom of the hill I was on my hands and knees in the rough stones when Donna ran to get me.

'Oh for Christ's sake! – Did you cut yourself? Are you bleeding?'

She examined me, making a face. She touched my knee where it was bleeding.

'It isn't anything,' she said.

I wasn't crying.

'It's just a little scratch,' she said angrily. 'You're always falling down, stupid little goddam baby, why can't you keep from falling down— She fell down, she cut her knee,' Donna told Albert, disgusted.

'I'm all right,' I said.

I was still trembling, the giant woman had frightened me so that nothing else mattered.

'Are you going to tell?' Albert asked.

'She won't tell,' Donna said.

'Are you—?'

'No.'

'She won't tell, she wouldn't dare,' Donna said.

'Old Mrs Mueller will call the police on you,' Albert said to me. 'You heard her, huh? She's going to call the police on you, you're the one she saw, she knows your name and—'

'Oh shut up,' Donna said. 'She doesn't know anybody's name. She's crazy. Don't get the baby started.'

'—really mad, wasn't she? Said something about killing us! The old bag! The old witch! Must have been hiding in there, in the coal shed. She must have been waiting for us. She's crazy, isn't she?'

'She isn't the only one,' Donna sang out.

Many years ago, in the foothills of the Chautauqua Mountains, where the north fork of the Eden River flows into the wide, flat, shallow Yew Creek, there lived a giant woman.

A wide face, brown and leathery, wrinkled as an old glove. A head that seemed enormous, too heavy for her thin neck; and the gray hair wild and frizzed about it. Shoulders broad as a man's. The chest sunken with age but the stomach and hips mammoth, flabby, and the thin, dead-white legs still muscular. . . . Sometimes she was seen walking along the road, as far away as Rockland, fifteen miles to the south; a few times we saw her in the little town of Derby, eighteen miles away, walking quickly along, her head down, muttering to herself. She usually carried bundles of some kind, and a satchel that seemed to be made of canvas. At such times she might glance up as ordinary people do – quizzical, attentive – and the eyes in that broad, big face were shiny-black, round, slightly protruding. Her expression would shift into a look of wonder and expectation. But then, for some reason, the eyes narrowed to slits, the face closed, stiffened, the line of the mouth became contemptuous and jeering, and she would mutter something inaudible.

'She hates us. She's always yelling at us. Why does she hate us?' I asked.

'She's no harm, is she?' my father said. He helped my mother with the wash, hanging the heavy things on the line, careful that the sheets and quilts did not touch the ground. My mother was pregnant. That was the summer she was pregnant for the fifth time. The baby was to be Jordan, the last child in the family. 'She's no harm to you, is she, just stay away from her, let her be, she's older than your grandmother – she won't hurt any of you.'

'Why does she hate us?'

'She hates everyone,' he said indifferently. 'She can't help it.'

She lived alone in a decaying farmhouse. She had sold off most of her land, had only a few acres now, kept to herself and rejected any of her neighbors' offers of help. She never spoke to anyone; she simply signalled angry dismissal. No shouting at adults. Only her big arms folded across her breasts, her head jerking from side to side, an inaudible mutter that might have been in a foreign language or in no language at all.

'Why does she live alone? Isn't she afraid to live alone?'

'Why does she live back there, so far from the road?'

'Why does she hate us . . .?'

None of the roads in our part of the county were paved then. But the road she lived on dwindled into a mere lane, a cow path, that was muddy in spring and, in winter, impassable for weeks at a time. The snow could drift as high as twelve feet, blown into odd, slanted mountains and valleys, fanning out from the oaks and sycamores that lined the lane, and no snowplows bothered with it. The road hadn't even a name, people referred to it as the 'Mueller Road,' but it had no name, no signpost.

'Why won't she let us cross her property?'

'She's old, she's sick, she's not like other people, don't ask so many questions,' they said.

I did not tell them about Donna and Albert and me.

'What if she dies, way back there? Wouldn't she be afraid, all alone? How could there be a funeral for her, how would people know about it . . .?'

'That's nobody's business, what she wants to do.'

'Wouldn't she be afraid . . .?'

'She isn't afraid of anything.'

People told stories about her; there were people who knew more than my parents, even my grandmother knew more. They said she had let someone die. They said she was like a murderer. It was the same as murder, wasn't it, what she had done . . .? Donna said it was her little boy, just my age; the old woman had let him die somehow and hadn't even told people about it, the way you are supposed to notify the doctor and the sheriff and other people in town when something bad happens . . . she had let the little boy die, a five-year-old boy, and then she had buried him herself. Dug the grave at the end of the cornfield, down the hill from the back of her house, and put the little boy in it and covered him up with dirt. . . . 'That's what she'll do to you, if she catches you,' Donna said suddenly. 'She'll dig a grave and push you in and fill it up again with that nasty dried-up old dirt—'

But I didn't cry, I wasn't going to cry. I wasn't afraid.

They said other things, different things. The little boy had not been Mrs Mueller's own son. Donna was wrong – she hadn't even been born yet, she had heard the story wrong, had mixed things up. Twelve years old and big for her age, noisy and tough as any of the boys, but not too bright – so people in the family said, behind my parents' backs – she forgot important things and remembered small things, mixed up names, became red-faced and angry when mistakes were pointed out to her. I pretended to agree with her so that she wouldn't slap me or pinch my arm. I tried not to cry if she ignored me. But I didn't trust her to tell the truth, to know how the truth really went.

No, the little boy had been Mrs Mueller's daughter's son. And Mr Mueller had been alive then. It was true that they had let the boy die – and Mrs Mueller had tried to bury him, had carried him down to the cornfield and was digging a grave for him, but the ground was too hard, it was still frozen, and she couldn't get the scoop of the shovel into it very deep.

But no: evidently that was just a rumor. A lie. There had been digging of a kind in the field, but it had nothing to do with the child, it hadn't been intended for a grave. There was no grave. Mrs Mueller had not tried to bury him. He had died in late winter, in March, and they hadn't known what to do with him – with the body – so they carried it out to a corncrib and left it there, under some tarpaulin. Where had the story come from, about the grave? And Mrs Mueller carrying the boy out to bury him?

After the boy died, the old couple were afraid to call a doctor. They believed they would be arrested and put in jail over in Rockland, where there was a state prison. Mr Mueller couldn't speak English – knew only a few words – had been always shy of going to town, of dealing with suppliers and shopkeepers. Mrs Mueller had done all the shopping. People laughed at them both. But they were intimidated by Mrs Mueller because she was so big, at least six feet five inches tall, must have weighed nearly two hundred fifty pounds at her heaviest, so people said, before she started to waste away. . . . The old man, when had he died? Six years ago? Seven? No, at least ten. He had died working his team of horses, only a few months after the little boy's death. Heat exhaustion, people said. Or a stroke. Or a heart attack.

People whispered: 'She let her little boy die because they were too cheap to call a doctor.'

They said: 'She worked her husband to death.'

And: 'They didn't put her in jail – just why was that?'

Sometimes they tapped their foreheads, meaning the old woman was crazy. Sometimes they said she wasn't crazy, but very shrewd, very cunning, only pretending to be crazy so that people would leave her alone. She had money hidden back there – no doubt about it. People like her, dressed in rags, always filthy, too cheap to keep up their houses and outbuildings, too cheap even to buy medicine when it was needed – why, people like that always had money hidden away. They were shrewd, cunning, evil.

What about the daughter?

People were less certain about her. She was 'no good', of course.

She had run away from home many years ago – many, many years ago. No one really remembered her. It was said that she ran away with a farm worker, a seasonal worker at one of the big farms, but it was sometimes said that Mrs Mueller had kicked her out – had beaten her with a broom – had blackened one of her eyes. She had been a bad girl, she'd been 'no good', 'wild', 'lazy'. But no one remembered her, only the old people, and they disagreed with one another. My grandmother and her friends sat on the porch and plucked memories out of the past with a strange myopic intensity, really indifferent to one another. They needed one another's company, there was a hunger for company, and yet when they began to talk each seemed to speak to herself, unaware of the others. I sat on the steps playing with the kittens, listening. Or flicking pebbles toward the chickens, to make them think it was feeding time, to get their attention. Sometimes I sat with my arms right around my knees, listening, not quite understanding what the old women were saying, just sitting there and listening, as if there were a truth that might suddenly become illuminated, though the old women themselves would not have realized it.

'. . . was working up at the train depot, they said. In the restaurant, so she could meet all kinds of men. They said she was married. . . .'

'She was never married! Who said—!'

'. . . but that was a lie, she just came back here on Sunday with the baby and left him with her parents, and that was that. Mrs Mueller had to keep him – what could she do? I never talked with her myself, I never visited with her myself but. . . .'

'They hid away back there. They were both crazy.'

'How much money do you think she's got?'

'. . . then the little boy got sick. And they wouldn't call a doctor of course. They didn't want to spend the money.'

'It was in the lungs, what do you call it—'

'Pneumonia.'

'They said it was just a bad cold. It was the end of winter, the snow was melting, they could have gotten a doctor without any trouble . . . could have come to us and we'd gotten him . . . but they were too cheap, cheap and nasty and mean. So the little boy died.'

'Blond curls all over his head, a beautiful little boy.'

'He was *not*. A little dark-faced wizened thing, like a monkey.

They never fed him – they were too cheap. Somebody said he was just skin and bones, and his teeth were all rotted, so young. Baby teeth all rotted in his head.'

'. . . had some Negro blood in him, maybe. That was the reason for. . . .'

'They said it was just a bad cold, just a touch of the flu. It was in his lungs, then went to his stomach and bowels, and food wouldn't stay in him, he just emptied himself out, was passing blood too, they said there wasn't time enough for a doctor. But they were too cheap anyway: they saved every penny they could.'

'It was pneumonia. He just choked to death, couldn't breathe.'

'. . . just to save money!'

'Or maybe to get rid of him, to have one less mouth to feed. I wouldn't put it past them.'

'*Her*, you mean.'

'Do you think . . .? Do . . .?'

'Why, you said that yourself! More than once!'

'I never. . . .'

Our property bordered her property in a swampy place. There was a marsh that dried out in summer, so that you could walk across it. I remember that rich sour stench; I remember getting dizzy from the stench, and being afraid of the marsh and liking it at the same time. I remember a special place inside a tall patch of cattails where I could crawl to hide; I remember crouching there and Mother running along the path only a few yards away, calling my name. 'Oh, where are you? Hon? Are you hiding around here? Are you all right? – Nothing's going to happen.'

Dragonflies. Frogs. Small yellow birds. The cicadas in the trees The heat of August mixed in with the smell of the marsh. There might have been garter snakes but I tried not to think about them. Sometimes I was afraid of the snakes, sometimes I wasn't.

I was afraid of the old woman.

I was afraid of her catching me by the hair – shaking me hard – the way they said she had grabbed a boy once.

Then there was Bobbie Orkin, who claimed she had crept up behind him, had grabbed him and screamed at him, said she would slit his throat like a chicken's, but he had kicked at her legs and gotten free . . . had picked up hunks of dried mud and thrown them at her and yelled back at her, saying he wasn't afraid. He had been exploring the Mueller's old hay barn, the big barn that had been hit by lightning a long time ago and wasn't used for anything now, not even storage, like other old, big barns on other farms in the area; he'd just been walking around in there, hadn't been doing anything wrong, and she had tried to kill him. So he said. But he'd thrown mud and stones at her, and shouted that he wasn't afraid of an ugly old warthog like her, and she'd better watch out or he'd come back at night and set fires. . . . He was thirteen years old but small for his age, wiry and fidgeting all the time, and you couldn't believe him; sometimes he lied and sometimes he told the truth and sometimes he got things mixed up in his own mind, and didn't know what he was saying.

No one would talk about her for months at a time. She was forgotten – just forgotten. Then they would happen to see her somewhere. They would say: She looks meaner than ever! She doesn't even look like a woman now! Then they would forget about her. But then, later, someone might say: How much money do you think she has, hidden away under her bed . . .?

Past the marsh was an old apple orchard. The Muellers had sold apples to a cider mill not far away, on the river, but that had been a long time ago – now the orchard was overgrown, the trees had not been pruned for years, the apples were tiny and hard and sour and worm-riddled. But we tried to eat them anyway – bit into them, then spat the pieces out in disgust. We picked up wind-fallen pears, turning them round and round to see how badly rotted they were or if there were worm- or insect-holes. And there were red currants, and huckleberries, and grapes that looked plump and sweet but were really bitter, so that we picked handfuls and threw them at one another. Everything had gone wild, like a jungle, like the banks of the creek where willow trees and bushes of all kinds grew so thick no one could keep a path clear for very long. There were flies and bees everywhere. And yellow jackets and wasps and hornets. And occasionally big birds, jays and grackles and starlings, even a few enormous crows, that hovered near us, tried to frighten us into leaving, shrieking and razzing us with their cries that were almost human. But we played in the orchard anyway. We tried to climb the trees, even the old, rotting pear trees, with no low branches to grab hold of, and sometimes part of an entire tree trunk would break off, the wood black and soft as flesh, running with tiny ants.

Once, we crept through the orchard . . . we approached the old woman's house . . . we hid behind an old woodpile where weeds had grown . . . we whispered together, frightened, excited, not knowing what would happen.

It was August. An afternoon in August.

I had not been near the house for a long time, no nearer than the orchard. Albert and Donna had gone exploring once, so they said, and had peeked into the old woman's kitchen window and even stepped into the shed, but I had not been with them. She hadn't been anywhere around, they said; nothing had happened, no one knew. That scrawny, ugly tiger-striped tom cat that had been bothering our cats and chickens was sleeping in the shed on a pile of rags – evidently *her* cat! Albert had clapped his hands to wake it, Donna had kicked at it, but the creature hadn't even been afraid – it hissed at them, ears laid back, eyes slits, it awoke immediately and in the same instant was ready to fight, a dirty nasty thing, Donna said, that should be killed. But it had escaped, it had run right past them and out the door.

They had run home, frightened by the cat.

No, Albert hadn't been frightened; he denied it. Donna had been the one. But she denied it too. She had heard something in the house – she thought – it might have been the old woman – sneaking up on them – maybe with a butcher knife or a hammer or a hand-scythe – you couldn't tell, she was crazy. So the two of them had run home, all the way home along the creek bank, panting and terrified, and afterward Donna had told me about it, because of the secret of whose cat that nasty cat was, but she said I mustn't tell anyone else, or I would get into trouble.

If they teased me when I followed them, if they pulled my hair and told me to go home, I didn't cry. I hid in certain places like the cattails and stayed by myself for a long time, sitting still, listening to the birds and insects, until I forgot about them and couldn't even remember what they had said or how delicate and painful the moment was when Donna could either grin and reach for my hand, and say I could come with them, or make a face at me and tell me to get back home where I belonged – I hid in the marsh or in one of the junked cars in the Wreszin's orchard and stayed by myself, sometimes crying a little, but most of the time just quiet, listening to the sounds outside me that were not Donna and Albert or anything human at all, until I felt very happy, and everything seemed all right again, and easy to live, and there was no problem or worry or fear, nothing at all, nothing bad that would last for very long – these things just went away, just vanished. They couldn't last.

But when I was with them again, I forgot and something changed in me, I wanted to follow them, I wanted to play with them, I forgot about being alone and being safe and quiet. I did things to make them tease me. Albert would pull my hair and tickle me so that it hurt; Donna would say I was fresh and wanted spanking, and was going to grow up worse than Ronnie – one of our grown-up cousins – who had been in trouble with the sheriff and had had to join the navy to keep from going to jail. . . . But they liked me better then. 'Can I come with you? Can I come with you?' I was always begging.

The shed stank.

They said it was spoiled food, maybe. Or maybe the cat had been bad in all those rags and papers.

'It smells like something dead,' Albert whispered.

'It does not! There's nothing dead in here!'

A raccoon could have crawled in here and died . . . a rabbit or a woodchuck or something. . . .'

Now the door to the kitchen, two steps up from the earthen floor of the shed.

There was a rusted screen door, the screen ripped and useless, and then a regular door. The spring of the screen door had broken. Donna opened the inner door slowly. She stood on her toes, on the step, and peered through the window of the door.

'You won't go in there,' Albert said. 'I bet you won't go in there.'

'If I go in, are you coming . . .?'

'*You* won't go in. You won't dare.'

'What about you?'

'Is the door locked? If it's locked. . . .'

But of course it wasn't locked. No one locked doors around here.

The kitchen: a surprise because it was bigger than ours at home. But it was an ugly place, the walls and ceiling dingy, the wood-burning stove blocking out light from one of the two narrow windows, big and black and ugly, made of iron. It was an old stove, my grandmother had had one like it, but my father had bought her a new one. We stood in the kitchen and were afraid to go forward or backward. 'What if she comes in from the shed . . .?' Albert whispered.

'She's out for all day,' Donna whispered. 'She was supposed to go to town, wasn't she. . . .'

'What if she comes back early?'

'Ma said she was due at the courthouse, something about taxes. She'd be in town for all day, she'd have to walk. . . . She won't be back early. You're just afraid.'

'I'm not afraid.'

They opened the cupboard doors but there was nothing interesting there – stacks of dishware, kettles, a platter made of white glass with scalloped edges, canisters like the ones we had at home, with *Flour* and *Sugar* and *Tea* on their fronts. The kitchen table had heavy legs with carved flowers on them, the kind of table you would expect to see in a living-room, and its surface was all scratches and burn marks. There were two chairs, one with a filthy cushion, the other used to set things on – cups, dishcloths or rags, a few knives and forks and spoons that seemed to be made of some dark, heavy, tarnished material, not like ours at home that were lightweight and stainless. These things were carved too and very grimy. The floor had no tile or linoleum, it was just bare floorboards, and you could smell the earth through them – the house had no cellar, just a crawl space.

They worked the hand pump at the sink. The first water that came out was tinged with rust.

I opened one of the doors on the stove – but it was just the place where wood and old newspapers were kept. Then I saw a spider. I slammed the door shut.

'How big a spider was it?' Donna asked. Her face crinkled; she hugged herself. Spiders frightened everyone in the family except the men – spiders even more than snakes.

'I closed the door on it,' I said. 'It can't get out.'

Albert and Donna went into the next room. It was a parlor, but very small. The shades were drawn, it was very hot and dusty. I was thinking of spiders and could feel things touching my bare legs, little pinpricks and itches. They went only a few steps into the room, then stopped. Albert glanced back over his shoulder and his face was pale and tight, a stranger's face. He looked at me almost without recognizing me. Donna giggled nervously. 'Jesus, it's hot in here. . . . What is that smell? Just dirt? Dust?' She punched one of the cushioned chairs and a cloud of dust exploded out of it. We all laughed.

They went into the last room, at the back of the house. I followed them, I was afraid to stay by myself. There were cobwebs everywhere, most of them broken and hanging in threads, blowing this way and that. Even on the globe of a kerosene lamp, where it would have been easy to wipe it away, there was part of a cobweb. Everything was silent except for us.

'So there are only three rooms in the house. . . .'

'It's bigger on the outside. It looks bigger on the outside.'

'There's no stairway. It must just be an attic up there and no way to get to it. . . . It's a sad, nasty place, isn't it?'

'I suppose you want to leave already!'

The back room was Mrs Mueller's bedroom. Blinds were drawn here, too, but it wasn't so dusty, you could see that someone lived in it. There was even a mirror with an old-fashioned ornate frame that could be tilted back and forth, however you wanted. Albert moved it a little and Donna poked him. 'Stop that! Don't you touch anything!'

'Go to hell,' Albert whispered. 'I'll do anything I want.'

'Don't you touch anything, I said!'

But he was already opening the drawers of the bureau – yanking them open one by one. The top drawer was filled with women's things, underclothes.

Donna was examining the bedspread. She didn't even notice what Albert had done. 'Hey, this is a fancy thing. She must have done this herself. It's all crochetwork, all these squares sewn together. It's pretty, it's nicer than Grandma's. But it's so old. . . .'

'Is this real gold?'

Albert held up a hairbrush

'It wouldn't be gold, it wouldn't be real,' Donna said.

There were things draped over chairs, pushed back in a corner. Clothes and sheets and towels. I couldn't tell if they were dirty or not. I lifted a blanket and found a black leather purse under it. 'Look what she found!' Albert said. But the purse was empty. It was very old, the catch was broken, it was empty except for a few hairpins and a rolled-up handkerchief.

'Look here,' Donna said.

She was squatting by the bed, had found a cardboard box under it. When she dragged it out, Albert said: 'Be careful!' because she almost ripped the sides. There were all sorts of papers in the box – letters still in envelopes – a book that must have been a Bible, with red-edged pages – but they were afraid to touch it, because of all the dustballs on top. She would know someone had been in her house.

'It's just some written stuff,' Albert said.

'There might be money. . . .'

'Yeah, but. . . .'

'You think she's got it hidden here, in here? Underneath this stuff?'

'Let me look.'

His hands were trembling. We all started to giggle.

It was too nervous for me, I couldn't watch him, I went to the window and peeked out – and it was a surprise, to see the Mueller's lane from here, from the inside of the house. I wondered if the old woman stood here sometimes, peeking around the shade, when people drove up the lane or when kids played out there. The lane looked so empty – someone could come at any time.

They were still looking through the box. They had found some old pictures, in frames, but didn't bother with them. 'This one's sort of cute,' Donna said indifferently. Brown-tinted, stiffly posed, a young couple with a baby – the man standing behind the woman, who sat on a straight-back chair, in a garden, holding an infant thickly wrapped in a long flowing white shawl. The man and the woman were young, very young, but the picture itself looked so old – their clothes were so old-fashioned – and it was strange, the stiffness of the pose, the dining-room chair out in a garden, the baby nearly lost in its blanket. I didn't want to look at it. I was very nervous; I started to giggle, though nothing was funny; I knew something bad might happen. Albert told me to shut up. His face was pale, so that his red-blond hair looked too bright. The way his mouth moved, the lips twitching while the teeth stayed clenched, was something I had never seen before.

'Go look through that bureau, get busy. We haven't got all day.'

I giggled. Then I stopped giggling. 'I want to go home,' I whispered.

'You heard me, get busy.'

'I want to go home. . . . I'm going home. . . .'

'You wait for us!' Donna said sharply.

Her voice was louder than Albert's, so loud it frightened us all.

I went to the bureau. It was a big piece of furniture, made of dark wood, not bright and polished like some of our furniture at home. On top was a soiled white cloth and the hairbrush and mirror and a few loose hairpins. They were the same kind my grandmother wore, made of thin wire, U-shaped, not the kind of pins my mother and sisters used. The bureau had carved drawers, but the designs were grimy – you couldn't tell what they were meant to be – and one of the cut-glass knobs was missing. I could see that the top drawer was filled with women's things, like my grandmother's underwear. I didn't want to look through it. I was afraid to look through it. So I eased the drawer shut, and Donna and Albert didn't notice. In the next drawer were linens. Pillowcases. They had yellowed, but the embroidered flowers and leaves on them were still white, smooth like satin or silk. I ran my thumb over them – it was strange to feel how smooth and clean they were.

A drop of water fell on the top pillowcase – it must have been sweat from my forehead. I wasn't crying.

I closed that drawer because there was nothing in it. I didn't need to look. The bottom drawer was jammed with woollens, I couldn't tell if they were large things like afghans or quilts, or shawls or sweaters. They were mostly dull colors – brown, olive green, black. It was a shame, how the moths had gotten them. I poked around in the bottom of the drawer and felt something hard. It was a book – a religious book – in a foreign language. It must have been in German. There were tiny gold crosses on the cover; the pages were very thin, almost transparent; in front there was a picture of Christ with a halo around his head and his heart flaming on the outside of his body. In back – In back there was money, slipped in sideways.

The bills were new, not like the dollar bills I was used to seeing, all wrinkled and dirty. These were stiff, they smelled new, though the other things in the drawer smelled so musty. I saw the numbers on the bills and my eyesight seemed to come and go, I blinked to get the sweat out of my eyes, I started to giggle and then stopped. I looked up, but there was nothing to see. The shade was drawn.

Around the edges of the shade the sunlight was very bright, but I couldn't see out the window.

'What's this?' Albert was saying to Donna. 'Can you read this?'

'. . . goddam junk.'

'What kind of stamps are these? A picture of a boat. . . .'

I couldn't make my eyes stay right. When I looked back at Albert and Donna, they were wavy, wobbly; they didn't seem like anyone I knew. They were squatting over the box, pawing through the things, panting, acting as if they were angry about something. They seemed to shift in and out of focus. . . . I felt very strange, the way I sometimes felt when I was alone, hiding, away from everyone else. I could see them, but they couldn't see me. Even when Donna glanced up to look at me, I felt that way.

'You done looking through that drawer . . .? Didn't you find anything either?'

I told her no. I closed the drawer. I told her no.

'Damn stupid waste of time, look, my hands are all dirty, I *told* you Mrs Mueller wouldn't have anything. . . .'

'You did not: it was your idea.'

'It wasn't! I said right away – what if we got caught? What if she came home?'

'You wanted to look around, you're always nosy. Probably stole something when nobody was looking. . . .'

'I did not! . . . Didn't want any of her old junk.'

They were still excited. Their voices were low and sharp at the same time, they didn't pay any attention to me.

'It's just as well. . . .' Donna said.

'She might have walked in the door and had a gun or something, she might have killed us. She's crazy. She could do anything. . . . It was your idea first of all.'

'I hope she doesn't figure out that somebody was in there. She might call the police and there'd be hell to pay. . . . It really stunk in there, didn't it?'

They giggled nervously.

They looked at me.

'. . . not going to tell, are you?'

I shook my head *no*.

'She won't tell,' Donna said. 'She isn't a tattle-tale.'

'She hadn't better tell,' Albert said.

'Oh leave her alone! ... You aren't going to tell, are you? Anyway, nothing happened. We didn't find anything and there's nothing to tell.'

They started running through the marsh. I let them run away, I fell behind, my face was burning and my eyes were sore and strange, as if I had been awake for a long time. I was very happy. I didn't know why: I was tired, I wanted to crawl on my mother's lap, I wanted to sleep or cry or. . . . I didn't know what I wanted or why I felt so happy.

They were by the creek bank now and their voices were too faint for me to hear. Suddenly I didn't care about them, I wasn't afraid of them, nothing would happen to me, nothing bad: their voices were so faint now that I hardly knew whose voices they were.

Next term, we'll mash you

Penelope Lively

Inside the car it was quiet, the noise of the engine even and subdued, the air just the right temperature, the windows tight-fitting. The boy sat on the back seat, a box of chocolates, unopened, beside him, and a comic, folded. The trim Sussex landscape flowed past the windows: cows, white-fenced fields, highly-priced period houses. The sunlight was glassy, remote as a coloured photograph. The backs of the two heads in front of him swayed with the motion of the car.

His mother half-turned to speak to him. 'Nearly there now, darling.'

The father glanced downwards at his wife's wrist. 'Are we all right for time?'

'Just right. Nearly twelve.'

'I could do with a drink. Hope they lay something on.'

'I'm sure they will. The Wilcoxes say they're awfully nice people. Not really the schoolmaster-type at all, Sally says.'

The man said, 'He's an Oxford chap.'

'Is he? You didn't say.'

'Mmn.'

'Of course, the fees are that much higher than the Seaford place.'

'Fifty quid or so. We'll have to see.'

The car turned right, between white gates and high, dark, tight-clipped hedges. The whisper of the road under the tyres changed to the crunch of gravel. The child, staring sideways, read black lettering on a white board: 'St Edward's Preparatory School. Please Drive Slowly'. He shifted on the seat, and the leather sucked at the bare skin under his knees, stinging.

The mother said, 'It's a lovely place. Those must be the playing-fields. Look, darling, there are some of the boys.' She clicked open her handbag, and the sun caught her mirror and flashed in the child's eyes; the comb went through her hair and he saw the grooves it left, neat as distant ploughing.

'Come on, then, Charles, out you get.'

The building was red brick, early nineteenth century, spreading out long arms in which windows glittered blackly. Flowers, trapped in neat beds, were alternate red and white. They went up the steps, the man, the woman, and the child two paces behind.

The woman, the mother, smoothing down a skirt that would be ridged from sitting, thought: I like the way they've got the maid all done up properly. The little white apron and all that. She's foreign, I suppose. Au pair. Very nice. If he comes here there'll be Speech Days and that kind of thing. Sally Wilcox says it's quite dressy – she got that cream linen coat for coming down here. You can see why it costs a bomb. Great big grounds and only an hour and a half from London.

They went into a room looking out into a terrace. Beyond, dappled lawns, gently shifting trees, black and white cows grazing behind iron railings. Books, leather chairs, a table with magazines – *Country Life, The Field, The Economist.* 'Please, if you would wait here. The Headmaster won't be long.'

Alone, they sat, inspected. 'I like the atmosphere, don't you, John?'

'Very pleasant, yes.' Four hundred a term, near enough. You can tell it's a cut above the Seaford place, though, or the one at St Albans. Bob Wilcox says quite a few City people send their boys here. One or two of the merchant bankers, those kind of people. It's the sort of contact that would do no harm at all. You meet someone, get talking at a cricket match or what have you . . . Not at all a bad thing.

'All right, Charles? You didn't get sick in the car, did you?'

The child had black hair, slicked down smooth to his head. His ears, too large, jutted out, transparent in the light from the window, laced with tiny, delicate veins. His clothes had the shine and crease of newness. He looked at the books, the dark brown pictures, his parents, said nothing.

'Come here, let me tidy your hair.'

The door opened. The child hesitated, stood up, sat, then rose again with his father.

'Mr and Mrs Manders? How very nice to meet you – I'm Margaret Spokes, and will you please forgive my husband who is tied up with some wretch who broke the cricket pavilion window and will be just a few more minutes. We try to be organised but a schoolmaster's day is always just that bit unpredictable. Do please sit down and what will you have to revive you after that beastly drive? You live in Finchley, is that right?'

'Hampstead, really,' said the mother. 'Sherry would be lovely.' She worked over the headmaster's wife from shoes to hairstyle, pricing and assessing. Shoes old but expensive – Russell and Bromley. Good skirt. Blouse could be Marks and Sparks – not sure. Real pearls. Super Victorian ring. She's not gone to any particular trouble – that's just what she'd wear anyway. You can be confident, with a voice like that, of course. Sally Wilcox says she knows all sorts of people.

The headmaster's wife said, 'I don't know how much you know about us? Prospectuses don't tell you a thing do they. We'll look round everything in a minute, when you've had a chat with my husband. I gather you're friends of the Wilcoxes, by the way. I'm awfully fond of Simon – he's down for Winchester, of course, but I expect you know that.'

The mother smiled over her sherry. Oh, I know that all right. Sally Wilcox doesn't let you forget that.

'And this is Charles? My dear, we've been forgetting all about you! In a minute I'm going to borrow Charles and take him off to meet some of the boys because after all you're choosing a school for him, aren't you, and not for you, so he ought to know what he might be letting himself in for and it shows we've got nothing to hide.'

The parents laughed. The father, sherry warming his guts, thought that this was an amusing woman. Not attractive, of course, a bit homespun, but impressive all the same. Partly the voice, of course; it takes a bloody expensive education to produce a voice like that. And other things, of course. Background and all that stuff.

'I think I can hear the thud of the Fourth Form coming in from games, which means my husband is on his way, and then I shall leave you with him while I take Charles off to the common room.'

For a moment the three adults centred on the child, looking, judging. The mother said, 'He looks so hideously pale, compared to those boys we saw outside.'

'My dear, that's London, isn't it? You just have to get them out, to get some colour into them. Ah, here's James. James – Mr and

Mrs Manders. You remember, Bob Wilcox was mentioning at Sports Day . . .'

The headmaster reflected his wife's style, like paired cards in Happy Families. His clothes were mature rather than old, his skin well-scrubbed, his shoes clean, his geniality untainted by the least condescension. He was genuinely sorry to have kept them waiting, but in this business one lurches from one minor crisis to the next . . . And this is Charles? Hello, there, Charles. His large hand rested for a moment on the child's head, quite extinguishing the thin, dark hair. It was as though he had but to clench his fingers to crush the skull. But he took his hand away and moved the parents to the window, to observe the mutilated cricket pavilion, with indulgent laughter.

And the child is borne away by the headmaster's wife. She never touches him or tells him to come, but simply bears him away like some relentless tide, down corridors and through swinging glass doors, towing him like a frail craft, not bothering to look back to see if he is following, confident in the strength of magnetism, or obedience.

And delivers him to a room where boys are scattered among inky tables and rungless chairs and sprawled on a mangy carpet. There is a scampering, and a rising, and a silence falling, as she opens the door.

'Now this is the Lower Third, Charles, who you'd be with if you come to us in September. Boys, this is Charles Manders, and I want you to tell him all about things and answer any questions he wants to ask. You can believe about half of what they say, Charles, and they will tell you the most fearful lies about the food, which is excellent.'

The boys laugh and groan; amiable, exaggerated groans. They must like the headmaster's wife: there is licensed repartee. They look at her with bright eyes in open, eager faces. Someone leaps to hold the door for her, and close it behind her. She is gone.

The child stands in the centre of the room, and it draws in around him. The circle of children contracts, faces are only a yard or so from him, strange faces, looking, assessing.

Asking questions. They help themselves to his name, his age, his school. Over their heads he sees beyond the window an inaccessible world of shivering trees and high racing clouds and his voice which has floated like a feather in the dusty schoolroom air dies altogether and he becomes mute, and he stands in the middle of them with shoulders humped, staring down at feet: grubby plimsolls and kicked brown sandals. There is a noise in his ears like rushing water, a torrential din out of which voices boom, blotting each other out so that he cannot always hear the words. Do you? they say, and Have you? and What's your? and the faces, if he looks up, swing into one another in kaleidoscopic patterns and the floor under his feet is unsteady, lifting and falling.

And out of the noises comes one voice that is complete, that he can hear. 'Next term we'll mash you', it says. 'We always mash new boys.'

And a bell goes, somewhere beyond doors and down corridors, and suddenly the children are all gone, clattering away and leaving him there with the heaving floor and the walls that shift and swing, and the headmaster's wife comes back and tows him away, and he is with his parents again, and they are getting into the car, and the high hedges skim past the car windows once more, in the other direction, and the gravel under the tyres changes to black tarmac.

'Well?'

'I liked it, didn't you?' The mother adjusted the car around her, closing windows, shrugging into her seat.

'Very pleasant, really. Nice chap.'

'I like him. Not quite so sure about her.'

'It's pricey, of course.'

'All the same . . .'

'Money well spent, though. One way and another.'

'Shall we settle it, then?'

'I think so. I'll drop him a line.'

The mother pitched her voice a notch higher to speak to the child in the back of the car. 'Would you like to go there, Charles? Like Simon Wilcox. Did you see that lovely gym, and the swimming-pool? And did the other boys tell you all about it?'

The child does not answer. He looks straight ahead of him, at the road coiling beneath the bonnet of the car. His face is haggard with anticipation.

The Exercise

Bernard Mac Laverty

'We never got the chance,' his mother would say to him. 'It wouldn't have done me much good but your father could have bettered himself. He'd be teaching or something now instead of serving behind a bar. He could stand up with the best of them.'

Now that he had started grammar school Kevin's father joined him in his work, helping him when he had the time, sometimes doing the exercises out of the text books on his own before he went to bed. He worked mainly from examples in the Maths and Language books or from previously corrected work of Kevin's. Often his wife took a hand out of him, saying 'Do you think you'll pass your Christmas Tests?'

When he concentrated he sat hunched at the kitchen table, his non-writing hand shoved down the back of his trousers and his tongue stuck out.

'Put that thing back in your mouth,' Kevin's mother would say, laughing. 'You've a tongue on you like a cow.'

His father smelt strongly of tobacco for he smoked both a pipe and cigarettes. When he gave Kevin money for sweets he'd say, 'You'll get sixpence in my coat pocket on the bannisters.'

Kevin would dig into the pocket deep down almost to his elbow and pull out a handful of coins speckled with bits of yellow and black tobacco. His father also smelt of porter, not his breath, for he never drank but from his clothes and Kevin thought it mixed nicely with his grown up smell. He loved to smell his pyjama jacket and the shirts that he left off for washing.

Once in a while Kevin's father would come in at six o'clock, sit in his armchair and say, 'Slippers'.

'You're not staying in, are you?' The three boys shouted and danced around, the youngest pulling off his big boots, falling back on the floor as they came away from his feet, Kevin, the eldest, standing on the arm of the chair to get the slippers down from the cupboard.

'Some one of you get a good shovel of coal for that fire,' and they sat in the warm kitchen doing their homework, their father reading the paper or moving about doing some job that their mother had been at him to do for months. Before their bedtime he would read the younger ones a story or if there were no books in the house at the time he would choose a piece from the paper. Kevin listened with the others although he pretended to be doing something else.

But it was not one of those nights. His father stood shaving with his overcoat on, a very heavy navy overcoat, in a great hurry, his face creamed thick with white lather. Kevin knelt on the cold lino of the bathroom floor, one elbow leaning on the padded seat of the green wicker chair trying to get help with his Latin. It was one of those exercises which asked for the nominative and genitive of: an evil deed, a wise father and so on.

'What's the Latin for "evil"?'

His father towered above him trying to get at the mirror, pointing his chin upwards scraping underneath.

'Look it up at the back.'

Kevin sucked the end of his pencil and fumbled through the vocabularies. His father finished shaving, humped his back and spluttered in the basin. Kevin heard him pull the plug and the final gasp as the water escaped. He groped for the towel then genuflected beside him drying his face.

'Where is it?' He looked down still drying slower and slower, meditatively until he stopped.

'I'll tell you just this once because I'm in a hurry.'

Kevin stopped sucking the pencil and held it poised, ready and wrote the answers with great speed into his jotter as his father called them out.

'Is that them all?' his father asked, draping the towel over the side of the bath. He leaned forward to kiss Kevin but he lowered his head to look at something in the book. As he rushed down the stairs he shouted back over his shoulder.

'Don't ever ask me to do that again. You'll have to work them out for yourself.'

He was away leaving Kevin sitting at the chair. The towel edged its way slowly down the side of the bath and fell on the floor. He got up and looked in the wash-hand basin. The bottom was covered in short black hairs, shavings. He drew a white path through them with his finger. Then he turned and went down the stairs to copy the answers in ink.

Of all the teachers in the school Waldo was the one who commanded the most respect. In his presence nobody talked, with the result that he walked the corridors in a moat of silence. Boys seeing him approach would drop their voices to a whisper and only when he was out of earshot would they speak normally again. Between classes there was always five minutes uproar. The boys wrestled over desks, shouted, whistled, flung books while some tried to learn their nouns, eyes closed, feet tapping to the rhythm of declensions. Others put frantic finishing touches to the last night's exercise. Some minutes before Waldo's punctual arrival, the class quietened. Three rows of boys, all by now strumming nouns, sat hunched and waiting.

Waldo's entrance was theatrical. He strode in with strides as long as his soutane would permit, his books clenched in his left hand and pressed tightly against his chest. With his right hand he swung the door behind him, closing it with a crash. His eyes raked the class. If, as occasionally happened, it did not close properly he did not turn from the class but backed slowly against the door snapping it shut with his behind. Two strides brought him to the rostrum. He cracked his books down with an explosion and made a swift palm upward gesture.

Waldo was very tall, his height being emphasised by the soutane, narrow and tight-fitting at the shoulders, sweeping down like a bell to the floor. A row of black gleaming buttons bisected him from floor to throat. When he talked his Adam's apple hit against the hard, white Roman collar and created in Kevin the same sensation as a fingernail scraping down the blackboard. His face was sallow and immobile. (There was a rumour that he had a glass eye but no-one knew which. Nobody could look at him long enough because to meet his stare was to invite a question.) He abhorred slovenliness. Once when presented with an untidy exercise book, dog-eared with a tea ring on the cover, he picked it up, the corner of one leaf between his finger and thumb, the pages splaying out like a fan, opened the window and dropped it three floors to the ground. His own neatness became exaggerated when he was at the board, writing in copperplate script just large enough for the boy in the back row to read – geometrical columns of declined nouns defined by exact, invisible margins. When he had finished he would set the chalk down and rub the used finger and thumb together with the same action he used after handling the host over the paten.

The palm upward gesture brought the class to its feet and they said the Hail Mary in Latin. While it was being said all eyes looked down because they knew if they looked up Waldo was bound to be staring at them.

'Exercises.'

When Waldo was in a hurry he corrected the exercises verbally, asking one boy for the answers and then asking all those who got it right to put up their hands. It was four for anyone who lied about his answer and now and then he would take spot checks to find out the liars.

'Hold it, hold it there,' he would say and leap from the rostrum, moving through the forest of hands and look at each boy's book, tracing out the answer with the tip of his cane. Before the end of the round and while his attention was on one book a few hands would be lowered quietly. Today he was in a hurry. The atmosphere was tense as he looked from one boy to another, deciding who would start.

'Sweeny, we'll begin with you.' Kevin rose to his feet, his finger trembling under the place in the book. He read the first answer and looked up at Waldo. He remained impassive. He would let someone while translating unseens ramble on and on with great imagination until he faltered, stopped and admitted that he didn't know. Then and only then would he be slapped.

'Two, nominative. *Sapienter Pater.*' Kevin went on haltingly through the whole ten and stopped, waiting for a comment from Waldo. It was a long time before he spoke. When he did it was with bored annoyance.

'Every last one of them is wrong.'

'But sir, Father, they couldn't be wr . . .' Kevin said it with such conviction, blurted it out so quickly that Waldo looked at him in surprise.

'Why not?'

'Because my . . .' Kevin stopped.

'Well?' Waldo's stone face resting on his knuckles. 'Because my what?'

It was too late to turn back now.

'Because my father said so,' he mumbled very low, chin on chest.

'Speak up, let us all hear you.' Some of the boys had heard and he thought they sniggered.

'Because my father said so.' This time the commotion in the class was obvious.

'And where does your father teach Latin?' There was no escape. Waldo had him. He knew now there would be an exhibition for the class. Kevin placed his weight on his arm and felt his tremble communicated to the desk.

'He doesn't, Father.'

'And what does he do?'

Kevin hesitated, stammering,

'He's a barman.'

'A barman!' Waldo mimicked and the class roared loudly.

'*Quiet.*' He wheeled on them. 'You, Sweeny. Come out here.' He reached inside the breast of his soutane and with a flourish produced a thin yellow cane, whipping it back and forth, testing it.

Kevin walked out to the front of the class, his face fiery red, the blood throbbing in his ears. He held out his hand. Waldo raised it higher, more to his liking, with the tip of the cane touching the underside of the upturned palm. He held it there for some time.

'If your brilliant father continues to do your homework for you, Sweeny, you'll end up a barman yourself.' Then he whipped the cane down expertly across the tips of his fingers and again just as the blood began to surge back into them. Each time the cane in its follow-through cracked loudly against the skirts of his soutane.

'You could have made a better job of it yourself. Other hand.' The same ritual of raising and lowering the left hand with the tip of the cane to the desired height. 'After all, I have taught you some Latin.' *Crack.* 'It would be hard to do any worse.'

Kevin went back to his place resisting the desire to hug his hands under his armpits and stumbled on a schoolbag jutting into the aisle as he pushed into his desk. Again Waldo looked round the class and said, 'Now we'll have it *right* from someone.'

The class continued and Kevin nursed his fingers, out of the fray.

As the bell rang Waldo gathered up his books and said, 'Sweeny, I want a word with you outside. Ave Maria, gratia plena . . .' It was not until the end of the corridor that Waldo turned to face him. He looked at Kevin and maintained his silence for a moment.

'Sweeny, I must apologise to you.' Kevin bowed his head. 'I meant your father no harm – he's probably a good man, a very good man.'

'Yes, sir,' said Kevin. The pain in his fingers had gone.

'Look at me when I'm talking, please.' Kevin looked at his collar, his Adam's apple, then his face. It relaxed for a fraction and Kevin thought he was almost going to smile, but he became efficient, abrupt again.

'All right, very good, you may go back to your class.'

'Yes Father,' Kevin nodded and moved back along the empty corridor.

Some nights when he had finished his homework early he would go down to meet his father coming home from work. It was dark, October, and he stood close against the high wall at the bus-stop trying to shelter from the cutting wind. His thin black blazer with the school emblem on the breast pocket and his short grey trousers, both new for starting grammar school, did little to keep him warm. He stood shivering, his hands in his trouser pockets and looked down at his knees which were blue and marbled, quivering uncontrollably. It was six o'clock when he left the house and he had been standing for fifteen minutes. Traffic began to thin out and the buses became less regular, carrying fewer and fewer passengers. There was a moment of silence when there was no traffic and he heard a piece of paper scraping along on pointed edges. He kicked it as it passed him. He thought of what had happened, of Waldo and his father. On the first day in class Waldo had picked out many boys by their names.

'Yes, I know your father well,' or 'I taught your elder brother. A fine priest he's made. Next.'

'Sweeny, Father.'

'Sweeny? Sweeny? – You're not Dr John's son, are you?'

'No Father.'

'Or anything to do with the milk people?'

'No Father.'

Twenty-five past six. Another bus turned the corner and Kevin saw his father standing on the platform. He moved forward to the stop as the bus slowed down. His father jumped lightly off and saw Kevin waiting for him. He clipped him over the head with the tightly rolled newspaper he was carrying.

'How are you big lad?'

'All right,' said Kevin shivering. He humped his shoulders and set off beside his father, bumping into him uncertainly as he walked.

'How did it go today?' his father asked.

'All right.' They kept silent until they reached the corner of their own street.

'What about the Latin?'

Kevin faltered, feeling a babyish desire to cry.

'How was it?'

'OK. Fine.'

'Good. I was a bit worried about it. It was done in a bit of a rush. Son, your Da's a genius.' He smacked him with the paper again. Kevin laughed and slipped his hand into the warmth of his father's overcoat pocket, deep to the elbow.

Bicycles, muscles, cigarets

Raymond Carver

It had been two days since Evan Hamilton had stopped smoking, and it seemed to him everything he'd said and thought for the two days somehow suggested cigarets. He looked at his hands under the kitchen light. He sniffed his knuckles and his fingers.

'I can smell it,' he said.

'I know. It's as if it sweats out of you,' Ann Hamilton said. 'For three days after I stopped I could smell it on me. Even when I got out of the bath. It was disgusting.' She was putting plates on the table for dinner. 'I'm so sorry, dear. I know what you're going through. But, if it's any consolation, the second day is always the hardest. The third day is hard, too, of course, but from then on, if you can stay with it that long, you're over the hump. But I'm so happy you're serious about quitting, I can't tell you.' She touched his arm. 'Now, if you'll just call Roger, we'll eat.'

Hamilton opened the front door. It was already dark. It was early in November and the days were short and cool. An older boy he had never seen before was sitting on a small, well-equipped bicycle in the driveway. The boy leaned forward just off the seat, the toes of his shoes touching the pavement and keeping him upright.

'You Mr Hamilton?' the boy said.

'Yes, I am,' Hamilton said. 'What is it? Is it Roger?'

'I guess Roger is down at my house talking to my mother. Kip is there and this boy named Gary Berman. It is about my brother's bike. I don't know for sure,' the boy said, twisting the handle grips, 'but my mother asked me to come and get you. One of Roger's parents.'

'But he's all right?' Hamilton said. 'Yes, of course, I'll be right with you.'

He went into the house to put his shoes on.

'Did you find him?' Ann Hamilton said.

'He's in some kind of jam,' Hamilton answered. 'Over a bicycle.

Some boy – I didn't catch his name – is outside. He wants one of us to go back with him to his house.'

'Is he all right?' Ann Hamilton said and took her apron off.

'Sure, he's all right.' Hamilton looked at her and shook his head. 'It sounds like it's just a childish argument, and the boy's mother is getting herself involved.'

'Do you want me to go?' Ann Hamilton asked.

He thought for a minute. 'Yes, I'd rather you went, but I'll go. Just hold dinner until we're back. We shouldn't be long.'

'I don't like his being out after dark,' Ann Hamilton said. 'I don't like it.'

The boy was sitting on his bicycle and working the handbrake now.

'How far?' Hamilton said as they started down the sidewalk.

'Over in Arbuckle Court,' the boy answered, and when Hamilton looked at him, the boy added, 'Not far. About two blocks from here.'

'What seems to be the trouble?' Hamilton asked.

'I don't know for sure. I don't understand all of it. He and Kip and this Gary Berman are supposed to have used my brother's bike while we were on vacation, and I guess they wrecked it. On purpose. But I don't know. Anyway, that's what they're talking about. My brother can't find his bike and they had it last, Kip and Roger. My mom is trying to find out where it's at.'

'I know Kip,' Hamilton said. 'Who's this other boy?'

'Gary Berman. I guess he's new in the neighborhood. His dad is coming as soon as he gets home.'

They turned a corner. The boy pushed himself along, keeping just slightly ahead. Hamilton saw an orchard, and then they turned another corner onto a dead-end street. He hadn't known of the existence of this street and was sure he would not recognize any of the people who lived here. He looked around him at the unfamiliar houses and was struck with the range of his son's personal life.

The boy turned into a driveway and got off the bicycle and leaned it against the house. When the boy opened the front door, Hamilton followed him through the living room and into the kitchen, where he saw his son sitting on one side of a table along with Kip Hollister and another boy. Hamilton looked closely at Roger and then he turned to the stout, dark-haired woman at the head of the table.

'You're Roger's father?' the woman said to him.

'Yes, my name is Evan Hamilton. Good evening.'

'I'm Mrs Miller, Gilbert's mother,' she said. 'Sorry to ask you over here, but we have a problem.'

Hamilton sat down in a chair at the other end of the table and looked around. A boy of nine or ten, the boy whose bicycle was missing, Hamilton supposed, sat next to the woman. Another boy, fourteen or so, sat on the draining board, legs dangling, and watched another boy who was talking on the telephone. Grinning slyly at something that had just been said to him over the line, the boy reached over to the sink with a cigaret. Hamilton heard the sound of the cigaret sputting out in a glass of water. The boy who had brought him leaned against the refrigerator and crossed his arms.

'Did you get one of Kip's parents?' the woman said to the boy.

'His sister said they were shopping. I went to Gary Berman's and his father will be here in a few minutes. I left the address.'

'Mr Hamilton,' the woman said, 'I'll tell you what happened. We were on vacation last month and Kip wanted to borrow Gilbert's bike so that Roger could help him with Kip's paper route. I guess Roger's bike had a flat tire or something. Well, as it turns out—'

'Gary was choking me, Dad,' Roger said.

'What?' Hamilton said, looking at his son carefully.

'He was choking me. I got the marks.' His son pulled down the collar of his T-shirt to show his neck.

'They were out in the garage,' the woman continued. 'I didn't know what they were doing until Curt, my oldest, went out to see.'

'He started it!' Gary Berman said to Hamilton. 'He called me a jerk.' Gary Berman looked toward the front door.

'I think my bike cost about sixty dollars, you guys,' the boy named Gilbert said. 'You can pay me for it.'

'You keep out of this, Gilbert,' the woman said to him.

Hamilton took a breath. 'Go on,' he said.

'Well, as it turns out, Kip and Roger used Gilbert's bike to help Kip deliver his papers, and then the two of them, and Gary too, they say, took turns rolling it.'

'What do you mean "rolling it"?' Hamilton said.

'Rolling it,' the woman said. 'Sending it down the street with a push and letting it fall over. Then, mind you – and they just admitted this a few minutes ago – Kip and Roger took it up to the school and threw it against a goalpost.'

'Is that true, Roger?' Hamilton said, looking at his son again.

'Part of it's true, Dad,' Roger said, looking down and rubbing his finger over the table. 'But we only rolled it once. Kip did it, then Gary, and then I did it.'

'Once is too much', Hamilton said. 'Once is one too many times, Roger. I'm surprised and disappointed in you. And you too, Kip,' Hamilton said.

'But you see,' the woman said, 'someone's fibbing tonight or else not telling all he knows, for the fact is the bike's still missing.'

The older boys in the kitchen laughed and kidded with the boy who still talked on the telephone.

'We don't know where the bike is, Mrs Miller,' the boy named Kip said. 'We told you already. The last time we saw it was when me and Roger took it to my house after we had it at school. I mean, that was the next to last time. The very last time was when I took it back here the next morning and parked it behind the house.' He shook his head. 'We don't know where it is,' the boy said.

'Sixty dollars,' the boy named Gilbert said to the boy named Kip. 'You can pay me off like five dollars a week.'

'Gilbert, I'm warning you,' the woman said. 'You see, *they* claim,' the woman went on, frowning now, 'it disappeared from *here*, from behind the house. But how can we believe them when they haven't been all that truthful this evening?'

'We've told the truth,' Roger said. 'Everything.'

Gilbert leaned back in his chair and shook his head at Hamilton's son.

The doorbell sounded and the boy on the draining board jumped down and went into the living room.

A stiff-shouldered man with a crew haircut and sharp gray eyes entered the kitchen without speaking. He glanced at the woman and moved over behind Gary Berman's chair.

'You must be Mr Berman?' the woman said. 'Happy to meet you. I'm Gilbert's mother, and this is Mr Hamilton, Roger's father.'

The man inclined his head at Hamilton but did not offer his hand.

'What's all this about?' Berman said to his son.

The boys at the table began to speak at once.

'Quiet down!' Berman said. 'I'm talking to Gary. You'll get your turn.'

The boy began his account of the affair. His father listened closely, now and then narrowing his eyes to study the other two boys.

When Gary Berman had finished, the woman said, 'I'd like to get to the bottom of this. I'm not accusing any one of them, you understand, Mr Hamilton, Mr Berman – I'd just like to get to the bottom of this.' She looked steadily at Roger and Kip, who were shaking their heads at Gary Berman.

'It's not true, Gary,' Roger said.

'Dad, can I talk to you in private?' Gary Berman said.

'Let's go,' the man said, and they walked into the living room.

Hamilton watched them go. He had the feeling he should stop them, this secrecy. His palms were wet, and he reached to his shirt pocket for a cigaret. Then, breathing deeply, he passed the back of his hand under his nose and said, 'Roger, do you know any more about this, other than what you've already said? Do you know where Gilbert's bike is?'

'No, I don't,' the boy said. 'I swear it.'

'When was the last time you saw the bicycle?' Hamilton said.

'When we brought it home from school and left it at Kip's house.'

'Kip,' Hamilton said, 'do you know where Gilbert's bicycle is now?'

'I swear I don't, either,' the boy answered. 'I brought it back the next morning after we had it at school and I parked it behind the garage.'

'I thought you said you left it behind the *house*,' the woman said quickly.

'I mean the house! That's what I meant,' the boy said.

'Did you come back here some other day to ride it?' she asked, leaning forward.

'No, I didn't,' Kip answered.

'Kip?' she said.

'I didn't! I don't know where it is!' the boy shouted.

The woman raised her shoulders and let them drop 'How do you know who or what to believe?' she said to Hamilton. 'All I know is, Gilbert's missing a bicycle.'

Gary Berman and his father returned to the kitchen.

'It was Roger's idea to roll it,' Gary Berman said.

'It was yours!' Roger said, coming out of his chair. 'You wanted to! Then you wanted to take it to the orchard and strip it!'

'You shut up!' Berman said to Roger. 'You can speak when spoken to, young man, not before. Gary, I'll handle this – dragged out at night because of a couple of roughnecks! Now if either of you,' Berman said, looking first at Kip and then Roger, 'know where this kid's bicycle is, I'd advise you to start talking.'

'I think you're getting out of line,' Hamilton said.

'What?' Berman said, his forehead darkening. 'And I think you'd do better to mind your own business!'

'Let's go, Roger,' Hamilton said, standing up. 'Kip, you come now or stay.' He turned to the woman. 'I don't know what else we can do tonight. I intend to talk this over more with Roger, but if there is a question of restitution I feel since Roger did help manhandle the bike, he can pay a third if it comes to that.'

'I don't know what to say,' the woman replied, following Hamilton through the living room. 'I'll talk to Gilbert's father – he's out of town now. We'll see. It's probably one of those things finally, but I'll talk to his father.'

Hamilton moved to one side so that the boys could pass ahead of him onto the porch, and from behind him he heard Gary Berman say, 'He called me a jerk, Dad.'

'He did, did he?' Hamilton heard Berman say. 'Well, he's the jerk. He looks like a jerk.'

Hamilton turned and said, 'I think you're seriously out of line here tonight, Mr Berman. Why don't you get control of yourself?'

'And I told you I think you should keep out of it!' Berman said.

'You get home, Roger.' Hamilton said, moistening his lips. 'I mean it,' he said, 'get going!' Roger and Kip moved out to the sidewalk. Hamilton stood in the doorway and looked at Berman, who was crossing the living room with his son.

'Mr Hamilton,' the woman began nervously but did not finish.

'What do you want?' Berman said to him. 'Watch out now, get out of my way!' Berman brushed Hamilton's shoulder and Hamilton stepped off the porch into some prickly cracking bushes. He couldn't believe it was happening. He moved out of the bushes and lunged at the man where he stood on the porch. They fell heavily onto the lawn. They rolled on the lawn, Hamilton wrestling Berman onto his back and coming down hard with his knees on the man's biceps. He had Berman by the collar now and began to pound his head against the lawn while the woman cried, 'God almighty, someone stop them! For God's sake, someone call the police!'

Hamilton stopped.

Berman looked up at him and said, 'Get off me.'

'Are you all right?' the woman called to the men as they separated. 'For God's sake,' she said. She looked at the men, who stood a few feet apart, backs to each other, breathing hard. The older boys had crowded onto the porch to watch; now that it was over, they waited, watching the men, and then they began feinting and punching each other on the arms and ribs.

'You boys get back in the house,' the woman said. 'I never thought I'd see,' she said and put her hand on her breast.

Hamilton was sweating and his lungs burned when he tried to take a deep breath. There was a ball of something in his throat so that he couldn't swallow for a minute. He started walking, his son and the boy named Kip at his sides. He heard car doors slam, an engine start. Headlights swept over him as he walked.

Roger sobbed once, and Hamilton put his arm around the boy's shoulders.

'I better get home,' Kip said and began to cry. 'My dad'll be looking for me,' and the boy ran.

'I'm sorry,' Hamilton said. 'I'm sorry you had to see something like that,' Hamilton said to his son.

They kept walking and when they reached their block, Hamilton took his arm away.

'What if he'd picked up a knife, Dad? or a club?'

'He wouldn't have done anything like that,' Hamilton said.

'But what if he had?' his son said.

'It's hard to say what people will do when they're angry,' Hamilton said.

They started up the walk to their door. His heart moved when Hamilton saw the lighted windows.

'Let me feel your muscle,' his son said.

'Not now,' Hamilton said. 'You just go in now and have your

dinner and hurry up to bed. Tell your mother I'm all right and I'm going to sit on the porch for a few minutes.'

The boy rocked from one foot to the other and looked at his father and then he dashed into the house and began calling, 'Mom! Mom!'

He sat on the porch and leaned against the garage wall and stretched his legs. The sweat had dried on his forehead. He felt clammy under his clothes.

He had once seen his father – a pale, slow-talking man with slumped shoulders – in something like this. It was a bad one, and both men had been hurt. It had happened in a café. The other man was a farmhand. Hamilton had loved his father and could recall many things about him. But now he recalled his father's one fistfight as if it were all there was to the man.

He was still sitting on the porch when his wife came out.

'Dear God,' she said and took his head in her hands. 'Come in and shower and then have something to eat and tell me about it. Everything is still warm. Roger has gone to bed.'

But he heard his son calling him.

'He's still awake,' she said.

'I'll be down in a minute,' Hamilton said. 'Then maybe we should have a drink.'

She shook her head. 'I really don't believe any of this yet.'

He went into the boy's room and sat down at the foot of the bed.

'It's pretty late and you're up, so I'll say good night,' Hamilton said.

'Good night,' the boy said, hands behind his neck, elbows jutting.

He was in his pajamas and had a warm fresh smell about him that Hamilton breathed deeply. He patted his son through the covers.

'You take it easy from now on. Stay away from that part of the neighborhood, and don't let me ever hear of you damaging a bicycle or any other personal property. Is that clear?' Hamilton said.

The boy nodded. He took his hands from behind his neck and began picking at something on the bedspread.

'Okay, then,' Hamilton said, 'I'll say good night.'

He moved to kiss his son, but the boy began talking.

'Dad, was Grandfather strong like you? When he was your age, I mean, you know, and you—'

'And I was nine years old? Is that what you mean? Yes, I guess he was,' Hamilton said.

'Sometimes I can hardly remember him', the boy said. 'I don't want to forget him or anything, you know? You know what I mean, Dad?'

When Hamilton did not answer at once, the boy went on. 'When you were young, was it like it is with you and me? Did you love him more than me? Or just the same?' The boy said this abruptly. He moved his feet under the covers and looked away. When Hamilton still did not answer, the boy said, 'Did he smoke? I think I remember a pipe or something.'

'He started smoking a pipe before he died, that's true,' Hamilton said. 'He used to smoke cigarets a long time ago and then he'd change brands and start in again. Let me show you something,' Hamilton said. 'Smell the back of my hand.'

The boy took the hand in his, sniffed it, and said, 'I guess I don't smell anything, Dad. What is it?'

Hamilton sniffed the hand and then the fingers. 'Now I can't smell anything, either,' he said. 'It was there before, but now it's gone.' Maybe it was scared out of me, he thought. 'I wanted to show you something. All right, it's late now. You better go to sleep,' Hamilton said.

The boy rolled onto his side and watched his father walk to the door and watched him put his hand to the switch. And then the boy said, 'Dad? You'll think I'm pretty crazy, but I wish I'd known you when you were little. I mean, about as old as I am right now. I don't know how to say it, but I'm lonesome about it. It's like – it's like I miss you already if I think about it now. That's pretty crazy, isn't it? Anyway, please leave the door open.'

Hamilton left the door open, and then he thought better of it and closed it halfway.

Red Dress – 1946

Alice Munro

My mother was making me a dress. All through the month of November I would come from school and find her in the kitchen, surrounded by cut-up red velvet and scraps of tissue-paper pattern. She worked at an old treadle machine pushed up against the window to get the light, and also to let her look out, past the stubble fields and bare vegetable garden, to see who went by on the road. There was seldom anybody to see.

The red velvet material was hard to work with, it pulled, and the style my mother had chosen was not easy either. She was not really a good sewer. She liked to make things; that is different. Whenever she could she tried to skip basting and pressing and she took no pride in the fine points of tailoring, the finishing of buttonholes and the overcasting of seams as, for instance, my aunt and my grandmother did. Unlike them she started off with an inspiration, a brave and dazzling idea; from that moment on, her pleasure ran downhill. In the first place she could never find a pattern to suit her. It was no wonder; there were no patterns made to match the ideas that blossomed in her head. She had made me, at various times when I was younger, a flowered organdie dress with a high Victorian neckline edged in scratchy lace, with a poke bonnet to match; a Scottish plaid outfit with a velvet jacket and tam; an embroidered peasant blouse worn with a full red skirt and black laced bodice. I had worn these clothes with docility, even pleasure, in the days when I was unaware of the world's opinion. Now, grown wiser, I wished for dresses like those my friend Lonnie had, bought at Beale's store.

I had to try it on. Sometimes Lonnie came home from school with me and she would sit on the couch watching. I was embarrassed by the way my mother crept around me, her knees creaking, her breath coming heavily. She muttered to herself. Around the house she wore no corset or stockings, she wore wedge-heeled shoes and ankle socks; her legs were marked with lumps of blue-green veins. I thought her squatting position shameless, even obscene; I tried to keep talking to Lonnie so that her attention would be taken away from my mother as much as possible. Lonnie wore the composed, polite, appreciative expression that was her disguise in the presence of grownups. She laughed at them and was a ferocious mimic, and they never knew.

My mother pulled me about, and pricked me with pins. She made me turn around, she made me walk away, she made me stand still. 'What do you think of it, Lonnie?' she said around the pins in her mouth.

'It's beautiful,' said Lonnie, in her mild, sincere way. Lonnie's own mother was dead. She lived with her father who never noticed her, and this, in my eyes, made her seem both vulnerable and privileged.

'It *will* be, if I can ever manage the fit,' my mother said. 'Ah, well,' she said theatrically, getting to her feet with a woeful creaking and sighing, 'I doubt if she appreciates it.' She enraged me, talking like this to Lonnie, as if Lonnie were grown up and I were still a child. 'Stand still,' she said, hauling the pinned and basted dress over my head. My head was muffled in velvet, my body exposed, in an old cotton school slip. I felt like a great raw lump, clumsy and goose-pimpled. I wished I was like Lonnie, light-boned, pale and thin; she had been a Blue Baby.

'Well nobody ever made me a dress when I was going to high school,' my mother said, 'I made my own, or I did without.' I was afraid she was going to start again on the story of her walking seven miles to town and finding a job waiting on tables in a boarding-house, so that she could go to high school. All the stories of my mother's life which had once interested me had begun to seem melodramatic, irrelevant, and tiresome.

'One time I had a dress given to me,' she said. 'It was a cream coloured cashmere wool with royal blue piping down the front and lovely mother-of-pearl buttons, I wonder what ever became of it?'

When we got free Lonnie and I went upstairs to my room. It was cold, but we stayed there. We talked about the boys in our class, going up and down the rows and saying, 'Do you like him? Well, do you half-like him? Do you *hate* him? Would you go out with him if he asked you?' Nobody had asked us. We were thirteen, and we had been going to high school for two months. We did questionnaires in

47

magazines, to find out whether we had personality and whether we would be popular. We read articles on how to make up our faces to accentuate our good points and how to carry on a conversation on the first date and what to do when a boy tried to go too far. Also we read articles on frigidity of the menopause, abortion and why husbands seek satisfaction away from home. When we were not doing school work, we were occupied most of the time with the garnering, passing on and discussing of sexual information. We had made a pact to tell each other everything. But one thing I did not tell was about this dance, the high school Christmas Dance for which my mother was making me a dress. It was that I did not want to go.

At high school I was never comfortable for a minute. I did not know about Lonnie. Before an exam, she got icy hands and palpitations, but I was close to despair at all times. When I was asked a question in class, any simple little question at all, my voice was apt to come out squeaky, or else hoarse and trembling. When I had to go to the blackboard I was sure – even at a time of the month when this could not be true – that I had blood on my skirt. My hands became slippery with sweat when they were required to work the blackboard compass. I could not hit the ball in volleyball; being called upon to perform an action in front of others made all my reflexes come undone. I hated Business Practice because you had to rule pages for an account book, using a straight pen, and when the teacher looked over my shoulder all the delicate lines wobbled and ran together. I hated Science; we perched on stools under harsh lights behind tables of unfamiliar, fragile equipment, and were taught by the principal of the school, a man with a cold, self-relishing voice – he read the Scriptures every morning – and a great talent for inflicting humiliation. I hated English because the boys played bingo at the back of the room while the teacher, a stout, gentle girl, slightly cross-eyed, read Wordsworth at the front. She threatened them, she begged them, her face red and her voice as unreliable as mine. They offered burlesqued apologies and when she started to read again they took up rapt postures, made swooning faces, crossed their eyes, flung their hands over their hearts. Sometimes she would burst into tears, there was no help for it, she had to run out into the hall. Then the boys made loud mooing noises; our hungry laughter – oh, mine too – pursued her. There was a carnival atmosphere of brutality in the room at such times, scaring weak and suspect people like me.

But what was really going on in the school was not Business Practice and Science and English, there was something else that gave life its urgency and brightness. The old building, with its rock-walled clammy basements and black cloakrooms and pictures of dead royalties and lost explorers, was full of the tension and excitement of sexual competition, and in this, in spite of daydreams of vast successes, I had premonitions of total defeat. Something had to happen, to keep me from that dance.

With December came snow, and I had an idea. Formerly I had considered falling off my bicycle and spraining my ankle and I had tried to manage this, as I rode home along the hard-frozen, deeply rutted country roads. But it was too difficult. However, my throat and bronchial tubes were supposed to be weak; why not expose them? I started getting out of bed at night and opening my window a little. I knelt down and let the wind, sometimes stinging with snow, rush in around my bared throat. I took of my pajama top. I said to myself the words "blue with cold" and as I knelt there, my eyes shut, I pictured my chest and throat turning blue, the cold, greyed blue of veins under the skin. I stayed until I could not stand it any more, and then I took a handful of snow from the windowsill and smeared it all over my chest, before I buttoned my pajamas. It would melt against the flannelette and I would be sleeping in wet clothes, which was supposed to be the worst thing of all. In the morning, the moment I woke up, I cleared my throat, testing for soreness, coughed experimentally, hopefully, touched my forehead to see if I had fever. It was no good. Every morning, including the day of the dance, I rose defeated, and in perfect health.

The day of the dance I did my hair up in steel curlers. I had never done this before, because my hair was naturally curly, but today I wanted the protection of all possible female rituals. I lay on the couch in the kitchen, reading *The Last Days of Pompeii*, and wishing I was there. My mother, never satisfied, was sewing a white lace collar on the dress; she had decided it was too grown-up looking. I watched the hours. It was one of the shortest days of the year. Above the couch, on the wallpaper, were old games of Xs and Os, old drawings and scribblings my brother and I had done when we were sick with bronchitis. I looked at them and longed to be back safe behind the boundaries of childhood.

When I took out the curlers my hair, both naturally and artificially stimulated, sprang out in an exuberant glossy bush. I wet it, I combed it, beat it with the brush and tugged it down along my cheeks. I applied face powder, which stood out chalkily on my hot face. My mother got out her Ashes of Roses Cologne, which she never used, and let me splash it over my arms. Then she zipped up the dress and turned me around to the mirror. The dress was princess style, very tight in the midriff. I saw how my breasts, in their new stiff brassiere, jutted out surprisingly, with mature authority, under the childish frills of the collar.

'Well I wish I could take a picture,' my mother said. 'I am really, genuinely proud of that fit. And you might say thank you for it.'

'Thank you,' I said.

The first thing Lonnie said when I opened the door to her was, 'Jesus, what did you do to your hair?'

'I did it up.'

'You look like a Zulu. Oh, don't worry. Get me a comb and I'll do the front in a roll. It'll look all right. It'll even make you look older.'

I sat in front of the mirror and Lonnie stood behind me, fixing my hair. My mother seemed unable to leave us. I wished she would. She watched the roll take shape and said, 'You're a wonder, Lonnie. You should take up hairdressing.'

'That's a thought,' Lonnie said. She had on a pale blue crepe dress, with a peplum and bow; it was much more grown-up than mine even without the collar. Her hair had come out as sleek as the girl's on the bobby-pin card. I had always thought secretly that Lonnie could not be pretty because she had crooked teeth, but now I saw that crooked teeth or not, her stylish dress and smooth hair made me look a little like a golliwog, stuffed into red velvet, wide-eyed, wild-haired, with a suggestion of delirium.

My mother followed us to the door and called out into the dark, 'Au reservoir!' This was a traditional farewell of Lonnie's and mine; it sounded foolish and desolate coming from her, and I was so angry with her for using it that I did not reply. It was only Lonnie who called back cheerfully, encouragingly, 'Good night!'

The gymnasium smelled of pine and cedar. Red and green bells of fluted paper hung from the basketball hoops; the high, barred windows were hidden by green boughs. Everybody in the upper grades seemed to have come in couples. Some of the Grade Twelve and Thirteen girls had brought boy friends who had already graduated, who were young businessmen around the town. These young men smoked in the gymnasium, nobody could stop them, they were free. The girls stood beside them, resting their hands casually on male sleeves, their faces bored, aloof and beautiful. I longed to be like that. They behaved as if only they – the older ones – were really at the dance, as if the rest of us, whom they moved among and peered around, were, if not invisible, inanimate; when the first dance was announced – a Paul Jones – they moved out languidly, smiling at each other as if they had been asked to take part in some half-forgotten childish game. Holding hands and shivering, crowding up together, Lonnie and I and the other Grade Nine girls followed.

I didn't dare look at the outer circle as it passed me, for fear I should see some unmannerly hurrying-up. When the music stopped I stayed where I was, and half-raising my eyes I saw a boy named Mason Williams coming reluctantly towards me. Barely touching my waist and my fingers, he began to dance with me. My legs were hollow, my arm trembled from the shoulder, I could not have spoken. This Mason Williams was one of the heroes of the school; he played basketball and hockey and walked the halls with an air of royal sullenness and barbaric contempt. To have to dance with a nonentity like me was as offensive to him as having to memorize Shakespeare. I felt this as keenly as he did, and imagined that he was exchanging looks of dismay with his friends. He steered me, stumbling, to the edge of the floor. He took his hand from my waist and dropped my arm.

'See you,' he said. He walked away.

It took me a minute or two to realize what had happened and that he was not coming back. I went and stood by the wall alone. The Physical Education teacher, dancing past energetically in the arms of a Grade Ten boy, gave me an inquisitive look. She was the only teacher in the school who made use of the words social adjustment, and I was afraid that if she had seen, or if she found out, she might make some horribly public attempt to make Mason finish out the dance with me. I myself was not angry or surprised at Mason; I accepted his position, and mine, in the world of school and I saw that what he had done was the realistic thing to do. He was a Natural Hero, not a Student Council type of hero bound for success beyond the school; one of those would have danced with me courteously and patronizingly and left me feeling no better off. Still, I hoped not many people had seen. I hated people seeing. I began to bite the skin on my thumb.

When the music stopped I joined the surge of girls to the end of the gymnasium. Pretend it didn't happen, I said to myself. Pretend this is the beginning, now.

The band began to play again. There was movement in the dense crowd at our end of the floor, it thinned rapidly. Boys came over, girls went out to dance. Lonnie went. The girl on the other side of me went. Nobody asked me. I remembered a magazine article Lonnie and I had read, which said *Be gay! Let the boys see your eyes sparkle, let them hear laughter in your voice! Simple, obvious, but how many girls forget!* It was true, I had forgotten. My eyebrows were drawn together with tension, I must look scared and ugly. I took a deep breath and tried to loosen my face. I smiled. But I felt absurd, smiling at no one. And I observed that girls on the dance floor, popular girls, were not smiling; many of them had sleepy, sulky faces and never smiled at all.

Girls were still going out to the floor. Some, despairing, went with each other. But most went with boys. Fat girls, girls with pimples, a poor girl who didn't own a good dress and had to wear a skirt and sweater to the dance; they were claimed, they danced away. Why take them and not me? Why everybody else and not me? I have a red velvet dress, I did my hair in curlers, I used a deodorant and put on cologne. *Pray*, I thought. I couldn't close my eyes but I said over and over again in my mind, *Please, me, please*, and I locked my fingers behind my back in a sign more potent than crossing, the same secret sign Lonnie and I used not to be sent to the blackboard in Math.

It did not work. What I had been afraid of was true. I was going to be left. There was something mysterious the matter with me, something that could not be put right like bad breath or overlooked like pimples, and everybody knew it, and I knew it; I had known it all along. But I had not known it for sure, I had hoped to be mistaken. Certainty rose inside me like sickness. I hurried past one or two girls who were also left and went into the girls' washroom. I hid myself in a cubicle.

That was where I stayed. Between dances girls came in and went out quickly. There were plenty of cubicles; nobody noticed that I was not a temporary occupant. During the dances, I listened to music which I liked but had no part of any more. For I was not going to try any more. I only wanted to hide in here, get out without seeing anybody, get home.

One time after the music started somebody stayed behind. She was taking a long time running the water, washing her hands, combing her hair. She was going to think it funny that I stayed in so long. I had better go out and wash my hands, and maybe while I was washing them she would leave.

It was Mary Fortune. I knew her by name, because she was an officer of the Girls' Athletic Society and she was on the Honour Roll and she was always organizing things. She had something to do with organizing this dance; she had been around to all the classrooms asking for volunteers to do the decorations. She was in Grade Eleven or Twelve.

'Nice and cool in here,' she said. 'I came in to get cooled off. I get so hot.'

She was still combing her hair when I finished my hands. 'Do you like the band?' she said.

'It's all right.' I didn't really know what to say. I was surprised at her, an older girl, taking this time to talk to me.

'I don't. I can't stand it. I hate dancing when I don't like the band. Listen. They're so choppy. I'd just as soon not dance as dance to that.'

I combed my hair. She leaned against a basin, watching me.

'I don't want to dance and don't particularly want to stay in here. Let's go and have a cigarette.'

'Where?'

'Come on, I'll show you.'

At the end of the washroom there was a door. It was unlocked and led into a dark closet full of mops and pails. She had me hold the door open, to get the washroom light, until she found the knob of another door. This door opened into darkness.

'I can't turn on the light or somebody might see,' she said. 'It's the janitor's room.' I reflected that athletes always seemed to know more than the rest of us about the school as a building; they knew where things were kept and they were always coming out of unauthorized doors with a bold, preoccupied air. 'Watch out where you're going,' she said. 'Over at the far end there's some stairs. They go up to a closet on the second floor. The door's locked at the top, but there's like a partition between the stairs and the room. So if we sit on the steps, even if by chance someone did come in here, they wouldn't see us.'

'Wouldn't they smell smoke?' I said.

'Oh, well. Live dangerously.'

There was a high window over the stairs which gave us a little light. Mary Fortune had cigarettes and matches in her purse. I had not smoked before except the cigarettes Lonnie and I made ourselves using papers and tobacco stolen from her father; they came apart in the middle. These were much better.

'The only reason I even came tonight,' Mary Fortune said, 'is because I am responsible for the decorations and I wanted to see, you know, how it looked once people got in there and everything. Otherwise why bother? I'm not boy-crazy.'

In the light from the high window I could see her narrow, scornful face, dark skin pitted with acne, her teeth pushed together at the front, making her look adult and commanding.

'Most girls are. Haven't you noticed that? The greatest collection of boy-crazy girls you could imagine is right here in this school.'

I was grateful for her attention, her company and her cigarette. I said I thought so too.

'Like this afternoon. This afternoon I was trying to get them to hang the bells and junk. They just get up on the ladders and fool around with boys. They don't care if it ever gets decorated. It's just an excuse. That's the only aim they have in life, fooling around with boys. As far as I'm concerned, they're idiots.'

We talked about teachers, and things at school. She said she wanted to be a physical education teacher and she would have to go to college for that, but her parents did not have enough money. She said she planned to work her own way through, she wanted to be independent anyway, she would work in the cafeteria and in the summer she would do farm work, like picking tobacco. Listening to her, I felt the acute phase of my unhappiness passing. Here was someone who had suffered the same defeat as I had – I saw that – but she was full of energy and self respect. She had thought of other things to do. She would pick tobacco.

We stayed there talking and smoking during the long pause in the music, when, outside, they were having doughnuts and coffee. When the music started again Mary said, 'Look, do we have to hang around here any longer? Let's get our coats and go. We can go down to Lee's and have a hot chocolate and talk in comfort, why not?'

We felt our way across the janitor's room, carrying ashes and cigarette butts in our hands. In the closet, we stopped and listened to make sure there was nobody in the washroom. We came back into the light and threw the ashes into the toilet. We had to go out and cut across the dance-floor to the cloakroom, which was beside the outside door.

A dance was just beginning. 'Go round the edge of the floor,' Mary said. 'Nobody'll notice us.'

I followed her. I didn't look at anybody. I didn't look for Lonnie. Lonnie was probably not going to be my friend any more, not as much as before anyway. She was what Mary would call boy-crazy.

I found that I was not so frightened, now that I had made up my mind to leave the dance behind. I was not waiting for anybody to choose me. I had my own plans. I did not have to smile or make signs for luck. It did not matter to me. I was on my way to have a hot chocolate, with my friend.

A boy said something to me. He was in my way. I thought he must be telling me that I had dropped something or that I couldn't go that way or that the cloakroom was locked. I didn't understand that he was asking me to dance until he said it over again. It was Raymond Bolting from our class, whom I had never talked to in my life. He thought I meant yes. He put his hand on my waist and almost without meaning to, I began to dance.

We moved to the middle of the floor. I was dancing. My legs had forgotten to tremble and my hands to sweat. I was dancing with a boy who had asked me. Nobody told him to, he didn't have to, he just asked me. Was it possible, could I believe it, was there nothing the matter with me after all?

I thought that I ought to tell him there was a mistake, that I was just leaving, I was going to have a hot chocolate with my girl friend. But I did not say anything. My face was making certain delicate adjustments, achieving with no effort at all the grave absent-minded look of these who were chosen, those who danced. This was the face that Mary Fortune saw, when she looked out of the cloakroom door, her scarf already around her head. I made a weak waving motion with the hand that lay on the boy's shoulder, indicating that I apologized, that I didn't know what had happened and also that it was no use waiting for me. Then I turned my head away, and when I looked again she was gone.

Raymond Bolting took me home and Harold Simons took Lonnie home. We all walked together as far as Lonnie's corner. The boys were having an argument about a hockey game, which Lonnie and I could not follow. Then we separated into couples and Raymond continued with me the conversation he had been having with Harold. He did not seem to notice that he was now talking to me instead. Once or twice I said, 'Well I don't know I didn't see that game,' but after a while I decided just to say 'H'm hmm,' and that seemed to be all that was necessary.

One other thing he said was, 'I didn't realize you lived such a long ways out.' And he sniffled. The cold was making my nose run a little too, and I worked my fingers through the candy wrappers in my coat pocket until I found a shabby Kleenex. I didn't know whether I ought to offer it to him or not, but he sniffled so loudly that I finally said, 'I just have this one Kleenex, it probably isn't even clean, it probably has ink on it. But if I was to tear it in half we'd each have something.'

'Thanks,' he said. 'I sure could use it.'

It was a good thing, I thought, that I had done that, for at my gate, when I said 'Well good night,' and after he said, 'Oh, yeah. Good night,' he leaned towards me and kissed me, briefly, with the air of one who knew his job when he saw it, on the corner of my mouth. Then he turned back to town, never knowing he had been my rescuer, that he had brought me from Mary Fortune's territory into the ordinary world.

I went around the house to the back door, thinking, I have been to a dance and a boy has walked me home and kissed me. It was all true. My life was possible. I went past the kitchen window and I saw my mother. She was sitting with her feet on the open oven door, drinking tea out of a cup without a saucer. She was just sitting and waiting for me to come home and tell her everything that had happened. And I would not do it, I never would. But when I saw the waiting kitchen, and my mother in her faded, fuzzy Paisley kimono, with her sleepy but doggedly expectant face, I understood what a mysterious and oppressive obligation I had, to be happy, and how I had almost failed it, and would be likely to fail it, every time, and she would not know.

Gold Dust

George Mackay Brown

'Is the post past?' said Bridie Kern to Mrs Scully. The garden-fence was between them. Mrs Scully was hanging up towels to dry. Streams of bright wind went over the council house gardens.

Mrs Scully removed two pegs from her teeth and said, 'I don't know.'

'Frankie's expecting a letter,' said Bridie Kern; as if the meagre intelligence was a spell or an intimation of immortality. 'The weed's expecting a letter,' said Mrs Scully to Mr Paton. 'What kind of letter would ever come to the likes of him?'

The garden-fence was between them.

Mr Paton was turning over his potato patch.

'His social security,' he said.

'His social security comes on a Friday,' said Mrs Scully. 'He's always up for *that*. He meets the postman half-way down the street.'

Mr Paton smiled and shook his head. He stuck his glittering spade in the earth.

Bridie Kern said in Somerville's, 'Ten tins of beer. It's for a party. A few of Frank's friends. Make it a dozen cans.'

'Frank's birthday?' said the licensed grocer.

'No, it isn't. It's a more important day than his birthday. It's never happened before. There'll be one or two red faces along Chapel Street when the word comes. Did you see the post?'

'Two pounds exactly,' said Mr Somerville.

'He's got himself a bird,' said Ida Innes the newsagent and tobacconist. 'He picked up some girl at the dance on Saturday. I saw them. There they were, standing in the door of the Freemasons'. I have to go up that close, you know, to get home. It was Frankie all right. I don't know who the bird was. Some lass from a farm, I think.'

'God help her,' said Mrs Scully, 'if she thinks that creature'll ever do anything for her.'

'He'll be expecting a love letter,' said Ida. '*The Daily News*, is it?'

'Love letter!' said Mrs Scully. 'Love letter! Do you think that trull of a mother of his would be treading the pavement like the Princess Royal all morning for that? Her paragon – sharing her paragon with another female.'

'You would have thought their mouths were stuck together,' said Ida Innes.

'I hear,' said Guthrie the scavenger, 'there's been money won on the pools along this street.'

'Is that so?' said the new young policeman.

'I know the fella to see,' said Guthrie. 'Doesn't have a job. Fred or Frank or some name. A right layabout. That's his mother, her with the bag of beer crossing the street.'

'If you win a big sum on the pools,' said Police-constable Stevenson, 'a telegram comes. Then a man flies up in a private plane from Liverpool.'

'It's just what I heard. Good luck to him,' said Guthrie.

'The post's taking a terrible time today,' said Bridie Kern to the tree in the presbytery garden. 'I wonder is he past? Frankie'll be that hurt if it doesn't come today. There'll be some red faces. None of them have had boys that were delicate from the time they were born. Frank'll be remembered when them and all their trash of sons and daughters are dust. They'll say, "Frank Kern was born in Chapel Street, in that house over there," in the years to come. . . .'

A blackbird in the priest's tree made response to Bridie Kern's pride with a burst of immaculate lyricism.

'I wonder,' said Bridie, 'should I knock on Father Macdonald's door and tell him? He'll be that pleased. I just know what he'll say. "Well, now, Bridie, I always knew the boy had something in him. A Robbie Burns for Alandale – well, well, well. And when will we be reading the poem? God bless you, now, Bridie. . . ." He's sure to say something like that. I would knock at the door, too, but there's that housekeeper of his taking cold looks at me from the edge of the curtain.'

'The worst thing that ever happened to the youth of this country,' said Mr Somerville to the man who was cleaning the street and the man who was preserving the queen's peace along Chapel Street and environs, 'the very worst thing, in my opinion, was when they abolished conscription. There's that poor woman, Bridie. She's out of her house every morning from before seven till after ten cleaning banks and offices, to keep that thing in idleness. A dozen cans of export, if you please. Some great word that's coming with the post. So poor Bridie can't go to her work this morning. (That's three pounds she's losing.) She must wait for this letter. The best letter that could ever be delivered to that young man would be from the Army, like in the old days, calling him up. They'd knock some sense into him there! They'd soon let him see what was what! There she is, the poor soul, peeping round the corner of Paterson's Close, seeing can she see the postman. And her owing more than five pounds from the weekend. Lord Muck must have his cigarettes and his Coca-Cola.'

'Good luck to him,' said Guthrie.

Eck Quoyle the postman turned out of Main Street at 10.41 a.m. precisely. He called at seven doors along Chapel Street, including a door marked *Miss Bridget Kern*. He dropped a large thick envelope through the letter-box. Then he walked briskly down the garden path and turned right at the corner and disappeared down Bank Street.

Francis Kern, a quarter of an hour or thereby later, carried the same large thick envelope (ravaged now at the flap) out through the front door of number 9 Chapel Street.

He walked slowly across the street towards 'The Lion of Scotland' bar.

His progress was observed from certain windows along both sides of the street: by Bridie Kern his mother, by Mrs Scully (widow), by Mr Thomas Paton (retired postal sorting clerk), by Mr Somerville the licensed grocer, by Mrs Ida Innes the newsagent and tobacconist, and by the priest's new nameless housekeeper from Uist.

Police-constable Stevenson had been summoned elsewhere by tinny noises on his 'walkie-talkie'.

Guthrie was turning into Aberavon Street when he saw from the corner of his eye the young man and the mysterious envelope. He began to sweep the pavement of Chapel Street for the second time in one morning, back towards the door of 'The Lion of Scotland' – a thing never known before.

It was five minutes after opening time that Frank Kern entered the bar. He was the first customer.

Frank asked for a pint of heavy.

While George the barman was drawing the beer Frank withdrew from the envelope what appeared to be a book or a catalogue. The title, in large crude smudgy type, was DIGGINGS – *A New Verse Quarterly*.

'What's this then?' said the barman. ('Twenty-five p.')

Frank, after consulting the page of contents, opened the magazine at another page. The paper had the texture of oatmeal. With his free hand Frank dredged coins out of his hip pocket and set them on the counter.

Mr Paton entered the bar: a thing never known before. (Mr Paton drank moderately, and in private, at home or in his friends' houses.)

Frank indicated to George an inch of cyclostyled type with his thumb. 'Something I've had published,' he said. 'A poem.'

The barman studied the page. Frank observed George over a thinning ellipse of foam. Mr Paton approached the counter, smiling.

At the doorway of 'The Lion of Scotland', neither out nor in, lingered Mrs Scully: a thing not known before. Mrs Scully was a great temperance woman.

George whistled. 'Is this you then, Frank? Did you write this?'

The poet nodded, gravely.

'Well done, Frank,' said George. 'I didn't know you went in for this sort of thing. Poetry, eh. Good luck anyway, pal.'

Guthrie's brush rasped the doorstep of 'The Lion of Scotland'. It drove Mrs Scully willy-nilly in across the threshold.

Mr Paton expressed interest. He asked if he might read the poem. He had always been interested in literature, he said. The magazine, open at the correct page, was passed across. Mr Paton studied Frank's poem for some time, his lips moving. At last he said it was good, in his opinion. Modern, of course, and difficult. No rhyme. You needed to read this kind of poetry a few times.

Frank lit a cigarette and drew the smoke deep into his lungs. He coughed twice into his clenched fist. Then he said, 'I'm busy on another poem. The editor wants more.'

'Can I get you something, madam?' called George the barman to Mrs Scully. Mrs Scully shook her head and looked confused: a thing hardly known before.

'I'll have a small vodka and orange,' said Mr Paton. 'Feel the need, after digging that garden. Your mother will be proud of you, Frank. Give Frank whatever he wants to drink, George.'

The scavenger had gone back to his trolly.

Bridie Kern could be seen on the opposite pavement, lingering and looking. (Like Mrs Scully she had never darkened the door of a public house in her life; nor would she, even on such a proud day.)

Mrs Scully was heard to whisper, 'He must have copied it out of some book.'

A pint of heavy beer, Mr Paton's tribute to literature, was set down in front of the poet.

The priest's housekeeper, a shopping basket in the crook of her arm, had stopped near Bridie on the street. They exchanged words (a thing not known till now). Bridie nodded her head, and smiled. The housekeeper gave one swift look into the dark interior of 'The Lion of Scotland', and passed on. Bridie lingered still, looking through the open door at the shadowy figures inside.

Mr Paton took a sip from his small glass of vodka and orange. He adjusted his spectacles. Once more he bent earnest brows upon the grey paper. He nodded once or twice.

Mrs Scully withdrew.

George asked Frank if there was much money in poetry. Frank looked grave. He raised his pint. He sent proud plumes of smoke down his nostrils.

Six coal miners came in and made for the counter, talking about horses and bets.

The curve of the poet's upper lip was richly crudded with foam.

Frank accepted the magazine from Mr Paton. He put it back quickly in its envelope, to be safe from the black hands of the miners.

Broken Homes

William Trevor

'I really think you're marvellous,' the man said.

He was small and plump, with a plump face that had a greyness about it where he shaved; his hair was grey also, falling into a fringe on his forehead. He was untidily dressed, a turtle-necked red jersey beneath a jacket that had a ballpoint pen and a pencil sticking out of the breast pocket. When he stood up his black corduroy trousers developed concertina creases. Nowadays you saw a lot of men like this, Mrs Malby said to herself.

'We're trying to help them,' he said, 'and of course we're trying to help you. The policy is to foster a deeper understanding.' He smiled, displaying small evenly-arranged teeth. 'Between the generations,' he added.

'Well, of course it's very kind,' Mrs Malby said.

He shook his head. He sipped the instant coffee she'd made for him and nibbled the edge of a pink wafer biscuit. As if driven by a compulsion, he dipped the biscuit into the coffee. He said:

'What age actually are you, Mrs Malby?'

'I'm eighty-seven.'

'You really are splendid for eighty-seven.'

He went on talking. He said he hoped he'd be as good himself at eighty-seven. He hoped he'd even be in the land of the living. 'Which I doubt,' he said with a laugh. 'Knowing me.'

Mrs Malby didn't know what he meant by that. She was sure she'd heard him quite correctly, but she could recall nothing he'd previously stated which indicated ill health. She thought carefully while he continued to sip at his coffee and attend to the mush of biscuit. What he had said suggested that a knowledge of him would cause you to doubt that he'd live to old age. Had he already supplied further knowledge of himself which, due to her slight deafness, she had not heard? If he hadn't, why had he left everything hanging in the air like that? It was difficult to know how best to react, whether to smile or to display concern.

'So what I thought,' he said, 'was that we could send the kids on Tuesday. Say start the job Tuesday morning, eh, Mrs Malby?'

'It's extremely kind of you.'

'They're good kids.'

He stood up. He remarked on her two budgerigars and the geraniums on her window-sill. Her sitting-room was as warm as toast, he said; it was freezing outside.

'It's just that I wondered,' she said, having made up her mind to say it, 'if you could possibly have come to the wrong house?'

'Wrong? *Wrong*? You're Mrs Malby, aren't you?' He raised his voice. 'You're Mrs Malby, love?'

'Oh, yes, it's just that my kitchen isn't really in need of decoration.'

He nodded. His head moved slowly and when it stopped his dark eyes stared at her from beneath his grey fringe. He said, quite softly, what she'd dreaded he might say: that she hadn't understood.

'I'm thinking of the community, Mrs Malby. I'm thinking of you here on your own above a greengrocer's shop with your two budgies. You can benefit my kids, Mrs Malby; they can benefit you. There's no charge of any kind whatsoever. Put it like this, Mrs Malby: it's an experiment in community relations.' He paused. He reminded her of a picture there'd been in a history book, a long time ago, History with Miss Deacon, a picture of a Roundhead. 'So you see, Mrs Malby,' he said, having said something else while he was reminding her of a Roundhead.

'It's just that my kitchen is really quite nice.'

'Let's have a little look, shall we?'

She led the way. He glanced at the kitchen's shell-pink walls, and at the white paintwork. It would cost her nearly a hundred pounds to have it done, he said; and then, to her horror, he began all over again, as if she hadn't heard a thing he'd been saying. He repeated that he was a teacher, from the school called the Tite Comprehensive. He appeared to assume that she wouldn't know the Tite Comprehensive, but she did: an ugly sprawl of glass and concrete buildings, children swinging along the pavements, shouting obscenities. The man repeated what he had said before about these children: that some of them came from broken homes. The ones he wished to send to her on Tuesday morning came from broken homes, which was no joke for them. He felt, he repeated, that we all had a special duty where such children were concerned.

Mrs Malby again agreed that broken homes were to be deplored. It was just, she explained, that she was thinking of the cost of decorating a kitchen which didn't need decorating. Paint and brushes were expensive, she pointed out.

'Freshen it over for you,' the man said, raising his voice. 'First thing Tuesday, Mrs Malby.'

He went away, and she realized that he hadn't told her his name. Thinking she might be wrong about that, she went over their encounter in her mind, going back to the moment when her doorbell had sounded. 'I'm from Tite Comprehensive,' was what he'd said. No name had been mentioned, of that she was positive.

In her elderliness Mrs Malby liked to be sure of such details. You had to work quite hard sometimes at eighty-seven, straining to hear, concentrating carefully in order to be sure of things. You had to make it clear you understood because people often imagined you didn't. Communication was what it was called nowadays, rather than conversation.

Mrs Malby was wearing a blue dress with a pattern of darker blue flowers on it. She was a woman who had been tall but had shrunk a little with age and had become slightly bent. Scant white hair crowned a face that was touched with elderly freckling. Large brown eyes, once her most striking feature, were quieter than they had been, tired behind spectacles now. Her husband, George, the owner of the greengrocer's shop over which she lived, had died five years ago; her two sons, Eric and Roy, had been killed in the same month – June 1942 – in the same desert retreat.

The greengrocer's shop was unpretentious, in an unpretentious street in Fulham called Agnes Street. The people who owned it now, Jewish people called King, kept an eye on Mrs Malby. They watched for her coming and going and if they missed her one day they'd ring her doorbell to see that she was all right. She had a niece in Ealing who looked in twice a year, and another niece in Islington, who was crippled with arthritis. Once a week Mrs Grove and Mrs Halbert came round with Meals on Wheels. A social worker, Miss Tingle, called; and the Reverend Bush called. Men came to read the meters.

In her elderliness, living where she'd lived since her marriage in

1920, Mrs Malby was happy. The tragedy in her life – the death of her sons – was no longer a nightmare, and the time that had passed since her husband's death had allowed her to come to terms with being on her own. All she wished for was to continue in these same circumstances until she died, and she did not fear death. She did not believe she would be re-united with her sons and her husband, not at least in a specific sense, but she could not believe, either, that she would entirely cease to exist the moment she ceased to breathe. Having thought about death, it seemed likely to Mrs Malby that after it came she'd dream, as in sleep. Heaven and hell were surely no more than flickers of such pleasant dreaming, or flickers of a nightmare from which there was no waking release. No loving omnipotent God, in Mrs Malby's view, doled out punishments and reward: human conscience, the last survivor, did that. The idea of a God, which had puzzled Mrs Malby for most of her life, made sense when she thought of it in terms like these, when she forgot about the mystic qualities claimed for a Church and for Jesus Christ. Yet fearful of offending the Reverend Bush, she kept such conclusions to herself when he came to see her.

All Mrs Malby dreaded now was becoming senile and being forced to enter the Sunset Home in Richmond, of which the Reverend Bush and Miss Tingle warmly spoke. The thought of a communal existence, surrounded by other elderly people, with sing-songs and card-games, was anathema to her. All her life she had hated anything that smacked of communal jolliness, refusing even to go on coach trips. She loved the house above the greengrocer's shop. She loved walking down the stairs and out on to the street, nodding at the Kings as she went by the shop, buying birdseed and eggs and fire-lighters, and fresh bread from Len Skipps, a man of sixty-two whom she'd remembered being born.

The dread of having to leave Agnes Street ordered her life. With all her visitors she was careful, constantly on the look-out for signs in their eyes which might mean they were diagnosing her as senile. It was for this reason that she listened so intently to all that was said to her, that she concentrated, determined to let nothing slip by. It was for this reason that she smiled and endeavoured to appear agreeable and co-operative at all times. She was well aware that it wasn't going to be up to her to state that she was senile, or to argue that she wasn't, when the moment came.

After the teacher from Tite Comprehensive School had left, Mrs Malby continued to worry. The visit from this grey-haired man had bewildered her from the start. There was the oddity of his not giving his name, and then the way he'd placed a cigarette in his mouth and had taken it out again, putting it back in the packet. Had he imagined cigarette smoke would offend her? He could have asked, but in fact he hadn't even referred to the cigarette. Nor had he said where he'd heard about her: he hadn't mentioned the Reverend Bush, for instance, or Mrs Grove and Mrs Halbert, or Miss Tingle. He might have been a customer in the greengrocer's shop, but he hadn't given any indication that that was so. Added to which, and most of all, there was the consideration that her kitchen wasn't in the least in need of attention. She went to look at it again, beginning to wonder if there were things about it she couldn't see. She went over in her mind what the man had said about community relations. It was difficult to resist men like that, you had to go on repeating yourself and after a while you had to assess if you were sounding senile or not. There was also the consideration that the man was trying to do good, helping children from broken homes.

'Hi,' a boy with long blond hair said to her on the Tuesday morning. There were two other boys with him, one with a fuzz of dark curls all round his head, the other red-haired, a greased shock that hung to his shoulders. There was a girl as well, thin and beaky-faced, chewing something. Between them they carried tins of paint, brushes, cloths, a blue plastic bucket, and a transistor radio. 'We come to do your kitchen out,' the blond boy said. 'You Mrs Wheeler then?'

'No, no. I'm Mrs Malby.'

'That's right, Billo,' the girl said. 'Malby.'

'I thought he says Wheeler.'

'Wheeler's the geyser in the paint shop,' the fuzzy-haired boy said.

'Typical Billo,' the girl said.

She let them in, saying it was very kind of them. She led them to the kitchen, remarking on the way that strictly speaking it wasn't in need of decoration, as they could see for themselves. She'd been thinking it over, she added: she wondered if they'd just like to wash the walls down, which was a task she found difficult to do herself?

They'd do whatever she wanted, they said, no problem. They put

67

their paint tins on the table. The red-haired boy turned on the radio. 'Welcome back to Open House,' a cheery voice said and then reminded its listeners that it was the voice of Pete Murray. It said that a record was about to be played for someone in Upminster.

'Would you like some coffee?' Mrs Malby suggested above the noise of the transistor.

'Great,' the blond boy said.

They all wore blue jeans with patches on them. The girl had a T-shirt with the words *I Lay Down With Jesus* on it. The others wore T-shirts of different colours, the blond boy's orange, the fuzzy one's light blue, the red-haired one's red. *Hot Jam-roll* a badge on the chest of the blond boy said; *Jaws* and *Bay City Rollers* other badges said.

Mrs Malby made them Nescafé while they listened to the music. They lit cigarettes, leaning about against the electric stove and against the edge of the table and against a wall. They didn't say anything because they were listening. 'That's a load of crap,' the red-haired boy pronounced eventually and the others agreed. Even so they went on listening. 'Pete Murray's crappy,' the girl said.

Mrs Malby handed them the cups of coffee, drawing their attention to the sugar she'd put out for them on the table, and to the milk. She smiled at the girl. She said again that it was a job she couldn't manage any more, washing walls.

'Get that, Billo?' the fuzzy-haired boy said. 'Washing walls.'

'Who loves ya, baby?' Billo replied.

Mrs Malby closed the kitchen door on them, hoping they wouldn't take too long because the noise of the transistor was so loud. She listened to it for a quarter of an hour and then she decided to go out and do her shopping.

In Len Skipps' she said that four children from the Tite Comprehensive had arrived in her house and were at present washing her kitchen walls. She said it again to the man in the fish shop and the man was surprised. It suddenly occurred to her that of course they couldn't have done any painting because she hadn't discussed colours with the teacher. She thought it odd that the teacher hadn't mentioned colours and wondered what colour the paint tins contained. It worried her a little that all that hadn't occurred to her before.

'Hi, Mrs Wheeler,' the boy called Billo said to her in her hall. He was standing there combing his hair, looking at himself in the mirror of the hall-stand. Music was coming from upstairs.

There were yellowish smears on the stair-carpet, which upset Mrs Malby very much. There were similar smears on the landing carpet. 'Oh, please, no!' she cried.

Yellow emulsion paint partially covered the shell-pink of one wall. Some had spilt from the tin on to the black-and-white vinyl of the floor and had been walked through. The boy with fuzzy hair was standing on a draining-board applying the same paint to the ceiling. He was the only person in the kitchen.

He smiled at Mrs Malby, looking down at her. 'Hi, Mrs Wheeler,' he said.

'But I said only to wash them,' she cried.

She feld tired, saying that. The upset of finding the smears on the carpets and of seeing the hideous yellow plastered over the quiet shell-pink had already taken a toll. Her emotional outburst had caused her face and neck to become warm. She felt she'd like to lie down.

'Eh, Mrs Wheeler?' The boy smiled at her again, continuing to slap paint on to the ceiling. A lot of it dripped back on top of him, on to the draining-board and on to cups and saucers and cutlery, and on to the floor. 'D'you fancy the colour, Mrs Wheeler?' he asked her.

All the time the transistor continued to blare, a voice inexpertly singing, a tuneless twanging. The boy referred to this sound, pointing at the transistor with his paint-brush, saying it was great. Unsteadily she crossed the kitchen and turned the transistor off. 'Hey, sod it, missus,' the boy protested angrily.

'I said to wash the walls. I didn't even choose that colour.'

The boy, still annoyed because she'd turned off the radio, was gesturing crossly with the brush. There was paint in the fuzz of his hair and on his T-shirt and his face. Every time he moved the brush about paint flew off it. It speckled the windows, and the small dresser, and the electric stove and the taps and the sink.

'Where's the sound gone?' the boy called Billo demanded, coming into the kitchen and going straight to the transistor.

'I didn't want the kitchen painted,' Mrs Malby said again. 'I told you.'

The singing from the transistor recommenced, louder than

before. On the draining-board the fuzzy-haired boy began to sway, throwing his body and his head about.

'Please stop him painting,' Mrs Malby shouted as shrilly as she could.

'Here,' the boy called Billo said, bundling her out on to the landing and closing the kitchen door. 'Can't hear myself think in there.'

'I don't want it painted.'

'What's that, Mrs Wheeler?'

'My name isn't Wheeler. I don't want my kitchen painted. I told you.'

'Are we in the wrong house? Only we was told—'

'Will you please wash that paint off?'

'If we come to the wrong house—'

'You haven't come to the wrong house. Please tell that boy to wash off the paint he's put on.'

'Did a bloke from the Comp come in to see you, Mrs Wheeler? Fat bloke?'

'Yes, yes, he did.'

'Only he give instructions—'

'Please would you tell that boy?'

'Whatever you say, Mrs Wheeler.'

'And wipe up the paint where it's spilt on the floor. It's been trampled out, all over my carpets.'

'No problem, Mrs Wheeler.'

Not wishing to return to the kitchen herself, she ran the hot tap in the bathroom on to the sponge-cloth she kept for cleaning the bath. She found that if she rubbed hard enough at the paint on the stair-carpet and on the landing carpet it began to disappear. But the rubbing tired her. As she put away the sponge-cloth, Mrs Malby had a feeling of not quite knowing what was what. Everything that had happened in the last few hours felt like a dream; it also had the feeling of plays she had seen on television; the one thing it wasn't like was reality. As she paused in her bathroom, having placed the sponge-cloth on a ledge under the hand-basin, Mrs Malby saw herself standing there, as she often did in a dream: she saw her body hunched within the same blue dress she'd been wearing when the teacher called, and two touches of red in her pale face, and her white hair tidy on her head, and her fingers seeming fragile. In a dream anything could happen next: she might suddenly find herself forty years younger, Eric and Roy might be alive. She might even be younger; Dr Ramsey might be telling her she was pregnant. In a television play it would be different: the children who had come to her house might kill her. What she hoped for from reality was that order be restored in her kitchen, that all the paint would be washed away from her walls as she had wiped it from her carpets, that the misunderstanding would be over. For an instant she saw herself in her kitchen, making tea for the children, saying it didn't matter. She even heard herself adding that in a life as long as hers you became used to everything.

She left the bathroom; the blare of the transistor still persisted. She didn't want to sit in her sitting-room, having to listen to it. She climbed the stairs to her bedroom, imagining the coolness there, and the quietness.

'Hey,' the girl protested when Mrs Malby opened her bedroom door.

'Sod off, you guys,' the boy with the red hair ordered.

They were in her bed. Their clothes were all over the floor. Her two budgerigars were flying about the room. Protruding from sheets and blankets she could see the boy's naked shoulders and the back of his head. The girl poked her face up from under him. She gazed at Mrs Malby. 'It's not them,' she whispered to the boy. 'It's the woman.'

'Hi there, missus.' The boy twisted his head round. From the kitchen, still loudly, came the noise of the transistor.

'Sorry,' the girl said.

'Why are they up here? Why have you let my birds out? You've no right to behave like this.'

'We needed sex,' the girl explained.

The budgerigars were perched on the looking-glass on the dressing-table, beadily surveying the scene.

'They're really great, them budgies,' the boy said.

Mrs Malby stepped through their garments. The budgerigars remained where they were. They fluttered when she seized them but they didn't offer any resistance. She returned with them to the door.

'You had no right,' she began to say to the two in her bed, but her voice had become weak. It quivered into a useless whisper, and once more she thought that what was happening couldn't be happening. She saw herself again, standing unhappily with the budgerigars.

In her sitting-room she wept. She returned the budgerigars to their cage and sat in an armchair by the window that looked out over Agnes Street. She sat in sunshine, feeling its warmth but not, as she might have done, delighting in it. She wept because she had intensely disliked finding the boy and girl in her bed. Images from the bedroom remained vivid in her mind. On the floor the boy's boots were heavy and black, composed of leather that did not shine. The girl's shoes were green, with huge heels and soles. The girl's underclothes were purple, the boy's dirty. There'd been an unpleasant smell of sweat in her bedroom.

Mrs Malby waited, her head beginning to ache. She dried away her tears, wiping at her eyes and cheeks with a handkerchief. In Agnes Street people passed by on bicycles, girls from the polish factory returning home to lunch, men from the brickworks. People came out of the greengrocer's with leeks and cabbages in baskets, some carrying paper bags. Watching these people in Agnes Street made her feel better, even though her headache was becoming worse. She felt more composed, and more in control of herself.

'We're sorry,' the girl said again, suddenly appearing, teetering on her clumsy shoes. 'We didn't think you'd come up to the bedroom.'

She tried to smile at the girl, but found it hard to do so. She nodded instead.

'The others put the birds in,' the girl said. 'Meant to be a joke, that was.'

She nodded again. She couldn't see how it could be a joke to take two budgerigars from their cage, but she didn't say that.

'We're getting on with the painting now,' the girl said. 'Sorry about that.'

She went away and Mrs Malby continued to watch the people in Agnes Street. The girl had made a mistake when she'd said they were getting on with the painting: what she'd meant was that they were getting on with washing it off. The girl had come straight downstairs to say she was sorry; she hadn't been told by the boys in the kitchen that the paint had been applied in error. When they'd gone, Mrs Malby said to herself, she'd open her bedroom window wide in order to get rid of the odour of sweat. She'd put clean sheets on her bed.

From the kitchen, above the noise of the transistor, came the clatter of raised voices. There was laughter and a crash, and then louder laughter. Singing began, attaching itself to the singing from the transistor.

She sat for twenty minutes and then she went and knocked on the kitchen door, not wishing to push the door open in case it knocked someone off a chair. There was no reply. She opened the door gingerly.

More yellow paint had been applied. The whole wall around the window was covered with it, and most of the wall behind the sink. Half of the ceiling had it on it; the woodwork that had been white was now a glossy dark blue. All four of the children were working with brushes. A tin of paint had been upset on the floor.

She wept again, standing there watching them, unable to prevent her tears. She felt them running warmly on her cheeks and then becoming cold. It was in this kitchen that she had cried first of all when the two telegrams had come in 1942, believing when the second one arrived that she would never cease to cry. It would have seemed ridiculous at the time, to cry just because her kitchen was all yellow.

They didn't see her standing there. They went on singing, slapping the paint-brushes back and forth. There'd been neat straight lines where the shell-pink met the white of the woodwork, but now the lines were any old how. The boy with the red hair was applying the dark-blue gloss.

Again the feeling that it wasn't happening possessed Mrs Malby. She'd had a dream a week ago, a particularly vivid dream in which the Prime Minister had stated on television that the Germans had been invited to invade England since England couldn't manage to look after herself any more. That dream had been most troublesome because when she'd woken up in the morning she'd thought it was something she'd seen on television, that she'd actually been sitting in her sitting-room the night before listening to the Prime Minister saying that he and the Leader of the Opposition had decided the best for Britain was invasion. After thinking about it, she'd established that of course it hadn't been true; but even so she'd glanced at the headlines of newspapers when she went out shopping.

'How d'you fancy it?' the boy called Billo called out to her, smiling across the kitchen at her, not noticing that she was upset. 'Neat, Mrs Wheeler?'

She didn't answer. She went downstairs and walked out of her hall-door, into Agnes Street and into the greengrocer's that had been her husband's. It never closed in the middle of the day; it never had. She waited and Mr King appeared, wiping his mouth. 'Well then, Mrs Malby?' he said.

He was a big man with a well-kept black moustache and Jewish eyes. He didn't smile much because smiling wasn't his way, but he was in no way morose, rather the opposite.

'So what can I do for you?' he said.

She told him. He shook his head and repeatedly frowned as he listened. His expressive eyes widened. He called his wife.

While the three of them hurried along the pavement for Mrs Malby's open hall-door it seemed to her that the Kings doubted her. She could feel them thinking that she must have got it all wrong, that she'd somehow imagined all this stuff about yellow paint and pop music on a radio, and her birds flying around her bedroom while two children were lying in her bed. She didn't blame them; she knew exactly how they felt. But when they entered her house the noise from the transistor could at once be heard.

The carpet of the landing was smeared again with the paint. Yellow footprints led to her sitting-room and out again, back to the kitchen.

'You bloody young hooligans,' Mr King shouted at them. He snapped the switch on the transistor. He told them to stop applying the paint immediately. 'What the hell d'you think you're up to?' he demanded furiously.

'We come to paint out the old ma's kitchen,' the boy called Billo explained, unruffled by Mr King's tone. 'We was carrying out instructions, mister.'

'So it was instructions to spill the blooming paint all over the floor? So it was instructions to cover the windows with it and every knife and fork in the place? So it was instructions to frighten the life out of a poor woman by messing about in her bedroom?'

'No one frightens her, mister.'

'You know what I mean, son.'

Mrs Malby returned with Mrs King and sat in the cubbyhole

behind the shop, leaving Mr King to do his best. At three o'clock he arrived back, saying that the children had gone. He telephoned the school and after a delay was put in touch with the teacher who'd been to see Mrs Malby. He made this telephone call in the shop but Mrs Malby could hear him saying that what had happened was a disgrace. 'A woman of eighty-seven,' Mr King protested, 'thrown into a state of misery. There'll be something to pay on this, you know.'

There was some further discussion on the telephone, and then Mr King replaced the receiver. He put his head into the cubbyhole and announced that the teacher was coming round immediately to inspect the damage. 'What can I entice you to?' Mrs Malby heard him asking a customer, and a woman's voice replied that she needed tomatoes, a cauliflower, potatoes and Bramleys. She heard Mr King telling the woman what had happened, saying that it had wasted two hours of his time.

She drank the sweet milky tea which Mrs King had poured her. She tried not to think of the yellow paint and the dark-blue gloss. She tried not to remember the scene in the bedroom and the smell there'd been, and the new marks that had appeared on her carpets after she'd wiped off the original ones. She wanted to ask Mr King if these marks had been washed out before the paint had had a chance to dry, but she didn't like to ask this because Mr King had been so kind and it might seem like pressing him.

'Kids nowadays,' Mrs King said. 'I just don't know.'

'Birched they should be,' Mr King said, coming into the cubbyhole and picking up a mug of the milky tea. 'I'd birch the bottoms off them.'

Someone arrived in the shop. Mr King hastened from the cubbyhole. 'What can I entice you to, sir?' Mrs Malby heard him politely enquiring and the voice of the teacher who'd been to see her replied. He said who he was and Mr King wasn't polite any more. An experience like that, Mr King declared thunderously, could have killed an eighty-seven-year-old stone dead.

Mrs Malby stood up and Mrs King came promptly forward to place a hand under her elbow. They went into the shop like that. 'Three and a half p,' Mr King was saying to a woman who'd asked the price of oranges. 'The larger ones at four.'

Mr King gave the woman four of the smaller size and accepted her money. He called out to a youth who was passing by on a bicycle, about to start an afternoon paper round. He was a youth who occasionally assisted him on Saturday mornings: Mr King asked him now if he would mind the shop for ten minutes since an emergency had arisen. Just for once, Mr King argued, it wouldn't matter if the evening papers were a little late.

'Well, you can't say they haven't brightened the place up, Mrs Malby,' the teacher said in her kitchen. He regarded her from beneath his grey fringe. He touched one of the walls with the tip of a finger. He nodded to himself, appearing to be satisfied.

The painting had been completed, the yellow and the dark-blue gloss. Where the colours met there were untidily jagged lines. All the paint that had been spilt on the floor had been wiped away, but the black-and-white vinyl had become dull and grubby in the process. The paint had also been wiped from the windows and from other surfaces, leaving them smeared. The dresser had been wiped down and was smeary also. The cutlery and the taps and the cups and saucers had all been washed and wiped.

'Well, you wouldn't believe it?' Mrs King exclaimed. She turned to her husband. However had he managed it all? she asked him. 'You should have seen the place!' she said to the teacher.

'It's just the carpets,' Mr King said. He led the way from the kitchen to the sitting-room, pointing at the yellow on the landing carpet and on the sitting-room one. 'The blooming stuff dried,' he explained, 'before we could get to it. That's where compensation comes in.' He spoke sternly, addressing the teacher. 'I'd say she has a bob or two owing.'

Mrs King nudged Mrs Malby, drawing attention to the fact that Mr King was doing his best for her. The nudge suggested that all would be well because a sum of money would be paid, possibly even a larger sum than was merited. It suggested also that Mrs Malby in the end might find herself doing rather well.

'Compensation?' the teacher said, bending down and scratching at the paint on the sitting-room carpet. 'I'm afraid compensation's out of the question.'

'She's had her carpets ruined,' Mr King snapped quickly. 'This woman's been put about, you know.'

'She got her kitchen done free,' the teacher snapped back at him.

'They released her pets. They got up to tricks in a bed. You'd no damn right—'

'These kids come from broken homes, sir. I'll do my best with your carpets, Mrs Malby.'

'But what about my kitchen?' she whispered. She cleared her throat because her whispering could hardly be heard. 'My kitchen?' she whispered again.

'What about it, Mrs Malby?'

'I didn't want it painted.'

'Oh, don't be silly now.'

The teacher took his jacket off and threw it impatiently on to a chair. He left the sitting-room. Mrs Malby heard him running a tap in the kitchen.

'It was best to finish the painting, Mrs Malby,' Mr King said. 'Otherwise the kitchen would have driven you mad, half done like that. I stood over them till they finished it.'

'You can't take paint off, dear,' Mrs King said, 'once it's on. You've done wonders, Leo,' she said to her husband. 'Young devils.'

'We'd best be getting back,' Mr King said.

'It's quite nice, you know,' his wife added. 'Your kitchen's quite cheerful, dear.'

The Kings went away and the teacher rubbed at the yellow on the carpets with her washing-up brush. The landing carpet was marked anyway, he pointed out, poking a finger at the stains left behind by the paint she'd removed herself with the sponge-cloth from the bathroom. She must be delighted with the kitchen, he said.

She knew she mustn't speak. She'd known she mustn't when the Kings had been there; she knew she mustn't now. She might have reminded the Kings that she'd chosen the original colours in the kitchen herself. She might have complained to the man as he rubbed at her carpets that the carpets would never be the same again. She watched him, not saying anything, not wishing to be regarded as a nuisance. The Kings would have considered her a nuisance too, agreeing to let children into her kitchen to paint it and then making a fuss. If she became a nuisance the teacher and the Kings would drift on to the same side, and the Reverend Bush would somehow be on that side also, and Miss Tingle, and even

77

Mrs Grove and Mrs Halbert. They would agree among themselves that what had happened had to do with her elderliness, with her not understanding that children who brought paint into a kitchen were naturally going to use it.

'I defy anyone to notice that,' the teacher said, standing up, gesturing at the yellow blurs that remained on her carpets. He put his jacket on. He left the washing-up brush and the bowl of water he'd been using on the floor of her sitting-room. 'All's well that ends well,' he said. 'Thanks for your cooperation, Mrs Malby.'

She thought of her two sons, Eric and Roy, not knowing quite why she thought of them now. She descended the stairs with the teacher, who was cheerfully talking about community relations. You had to make allowances, he said, for kids like that; you had to try and understand; you couldn't just walk away.

Quite suddenly she wanted to tell him about Eric and Roy. In the desire to talk about them she imagined their bodies, as she used to in the past, soon after they'd been killed. They lay on desert sand, desert birds swooped down on them. Their four eyes were gone. She wanted to explain to the teacher that they'd been happy, a contented family in Agnes Street, until the war came and smashed everything to pieces. Nothing had been the same afterwards. It hadn't been easy to continue with nothing to continue for. Each room in the house had contained different memories of the two boys growing up. Cooking and cleaning had seemed pointless. The shop which would have been theirs would have to pass to someone else.

And yet time had soothed the awful double wound. The horror of the emptiness had been lived with, and if having the Kings in the shop now wasn't the same as having your sons there at least the Kings were kind. Thirty-four years after the destruction of your family you were happy in your elderliness because time had been merciful. She wanted to tell the teacher that also, she didn't know why, except that in some way it seemed relevant. But she didn't tell him because it would have been difficult to begin, because in the effort there'd be the danger of seeming senile. Instead she said goodbye, concentrating on that. She said she was sorry, saying it just to show she was aware that she hadn't made herself clear to the children. Conversation had broken down between the children and herself, she wanted him to know she knew it had.

He nodded vaguely, not listening to her. He was trying to make the world a better place, he said, 'For kids like that, Mrs Malby. Victims of broken homes.'

KBW

Farrukh Dhondy

Tahir's gone now. No one to play chess with. I ask my dad for a game and he says he has a union meeting to attend this evening. 'Young Habib would've given you three in a row with one hand tied behind his blooming back,' he says as he goes out.

My dad says they're going to move an Irish family in. He knows that I shall miss Tahir. 'Maybe young Paddy will know some chess,' he says.

Their flat was exactly like ours, except the other way round, like when you see a thing in a mirror. Like twins growing out of each other our two flats were. And I was Tahir's best friend. The windows are still smashed, but the flat's been boarded up, like some others on our estate. It goes for kilometres. You must've heard of it, it's called the Devonmount Estate, Borough of Hackney. I shan't go to cricket practice today. I dropped out after Tahir left. We joined the team together so I think it's only right that we pull out together.

My mother don't understand. She says, 'Go on out and do something. Go and play cricket, you can't help the way the world is. Don't sit there looking like a month of wet Sundays'.

Dad understands. 'Son, you're right. Don't have no truck with racialist swine.' He always talks like that. Mum still needles him about being a Communist and he always replies that he's a Red in her bed, and the day she tries to put him under for his political views, he'll leave. They all know my dad on the estate. Twenty-two years he's been here.

I was born here and went to school here, to Devonmount Juniors and then Devonmount Comprehensive, no less. Tahir came here eight months ago. His dad came from Bangladesh, because they was driven out by the riots. That's what Tahir told me. He came straight into the fourth form. I took him to school the first day. My dad introduced hisself to Mr Habib as soon as they moved in, and he said to me at dinner that day, 'My boy, a Bengali family has moved in next door, and I've told mister that you are going to take master to school. He's in your school and I want you to take him in and stick him outside the Headmaster's office'.

That's how I met Tahir. I asked him what games he liked and he said cricket so I took him to Mr Hadley, the local vicar who runs the cricket team, and Tahir bowled for us. He was great. He lit up when they said they wanted to try him. Mr Hadley gave him the bat and bowled to him, and Tahir struck it hard to mid-off and was caught first go. Then Hadley gave him the ball. Tahir stroked it like it was a pigeon or something and when he looked up there was a shine in his eyes, same as you get out of the toe of a shoe when you put spit on the leather. He took a short run and bowled that ball. It spun at an amazing speed to leg-side.

'What do we have here?' Mr Hadley said, and his glasses gleamed. Tahir was our best spin bowler. He took four wickets in the match against the Mercer's Estate. When we won that match we were sure to get to the finals with the Atlanta Atlases. They were the best estate club going. If we beat them we'd be champs of Hackney. If you don't live in Hackney and don't live on the Devonmount, you don't know what that means. But I'll tell you what it means. It means Vietnam, North Vietnam that is, beating America in a war. That's what it means, a little country with a lot of determination, and without two ha'pennies to rub together, beating what my dad calls the biggest military machine ever built by man or money. Because ours is the worst estate. The flats are filthy and the stairs and the courtyard are never cleaned. There's coal dumps in the yards and half the places are boarded up. You should have seen the Habib's flat. Water pouring down the wall of one bedroom, the wallpaper all peeling off like scabs, and the roof-plaster all torn to bits. My dad said that it was nothing less than a crying shame for a workers' government to treat the workers so. My mum said she remembered when she was a little girl, and they ought to be thankful for a bathful of water which was hot.

The door of their flat has been forced open and the young ones play in there. That's what they call kids who still go to primary school on the Devonmount. I'm not a little 'un any more, I'm twelve and I'm not interested in climbing the garbage carts and pulling bits off people's cars and playing cowboys and Indians or hide and seek or cops and robbers in the empty flats. I used to be, and in those days I couldn't see why everyone on the estate complained about it. To me the empty flats were space. They gave you the feeling not that you belonged there, but that the place belonged to you so you could never leave it. Last year they built an adventure playground for the little 'uns on an empty site, and they went in hordes there, but after a while they didn't like it, they stopped going and started back in the empty flats again. There was nothing to nick in the adventure playground but the empties. You can find and flog all sorts of things around here. There are some blokes on the estate who'll give you quite a few pence for a load of pipes or even for boards and doorknobs and toilet seats and that, and the kids on the estate break in and rip everything up. It's only when a flat has been completely ripped up that it becomes a place to play in. It gets cleaned out like a corpse gutted by sharks. I walked through their flat yesterday and it's been done over.

When Tahir's family first moved in, the people around didn't like it. They didn't go to the trouble to worry them, but the boys from C Block came to our building and painted 'Niggers Out' on the landing. My dad said it was a shame and he gave me some turps and a rag and asked me to clean it off, but I couldn't, it wouldn't come off. He said it was an insult to coloureds, and I know it was because the lads from C Block don't like coloured people – they're always picking on Pakis and coons when they're in a gang. My mum says they only do it because they're really scared of them, but I don't think they are. When Tahir and I came home from school together they used to shout, 'Want to buy an elephant?' and all that bollocks. Tahir never took any notice. He always walked looking straight ahead, but even though he didn't understand what they were saying, he'd become very silent and not say a word to me all the rest of the way. I still think I was his best friend. There was always six of them and they was bigger than us. Sometimes they'd even come to our block and shout from downstairs. If Tahir's father heard them he'd come out on the gallery and shout back at them. I think he was a very brave man. He wasn't scared of anyone and he'd say, 'Get out, swine,' because those were the only swear words in English that he knew. He didn't speak English very much and when my dad met him on the stairs or invited him round for a cup of tea, he'd just say, 'It is very kind, don't trouble, please don't trouble'. Tahir told me once that his father was a karate expert and could break three bricks with one hand. And he was strong. One day when I was in their flat, he lifted a whole big refrigerator all by hisself from the bottom of the stairs.

The trouble all started with the newspapers. There was a story in the *Sun* one day which said that two people in London had died of typhoid. My mum and dad talked about it at home and Mrs Biggles, my mum's mate, said that a girl in C Block had been taken to St Margaret's Hospital and was under observation there. The girl was called Jenny and we knew her 'cause she used to go to the same school as my little sister Lynn.

The story went around the estate that there was typhus in the East End, and everybody was talking about it. Then a funny thing happened. We play cricket down in Haggerston Park and after the game, when Mr Hadley has locked the kit away in the hut at the corner, he takes us all to the vicarage and he gives us bags of crisps and cups of cocoa, and lets us listen to his records. Well, this last Saturday, we had a lot of kids turn up for cricket practice. Usually there's only the team, about thirteen lads, but this time there was eighteen because Mr Hadley said we had to have proper trials for the juniors team. We all sat around while James and Mr Hadley made the cocoa. He peeped around the door and said, 'There's only seven mugs, so you'll have to share the cocoa'.

We said, 'Right ho, umpire,' because that's what he likes to be called. Sometimes he tells us, if he's feeling like talking about church, that vicars are umpires from God and that life is like a test match between good and evil. I think Mr Hadley explains things well, but I still don't believe in it. My dad says that Hadley should stick to cricket and not brainwash the team, because my dad's dead against the Christians. He's an atheist but our mum tells us not to take any notice of him, because she believes in God.

Anyway, on this Saturday, James brought in the cups of cocoa to the team and gave them to every second person, as two people had to share. We were sitting in a circle on the carpet and Nick was changing the records. Every now and then someone would get up and there'd be an argument about whether to have David Essex or the Slade on next. Tahir never said a word. He was holding his steaming cup of cocoa and you could see the gaps in his teeth when he smiled. The lads would ask him to whistle and he'd always try but he couldn't do it on account of the big gap in his front teeth.

Next to Tahir there was a boy called Alan, and when Tahir had taken a few sips of the cocoa after it had cooled, he passed it on to him. The rest of us were fighting for the mugs, just mucking about sort of, and eating crisps at the same time. I was watching this boy Alan, who had freckles and a thin face which looked scared most of the time, and I could see that he didn't want to take the cup from Tahir.

'Have it, I've finished,' Tahir said.

Alan said he didn't want any cocoa, so Tahir turned to try and give the mug back to James.

'Everyone's got one,' James said. 'They're sharing if they haven't.'

'You didn't get,' Tahir said, smiling upward at James.

'I'll share someone's,' James replied, but when Tahir tried to give him his cup, he said, 'No, that's all right, you have the rest; I'll get some later'.

Tahir put his cup down in the middle of the carpet. All the cocoa from the other mugs was finished, but no one wanted to pick up Tahir's mug. Then it struck me. Mr Hadley shouted from the kitchen that the milk was finished, and there was a sort of silence in the room.

Tahir was searching the other faces. 'Anybody could drink it,' he said.

Nobody picked up the mug. It stood on the carpet, not even half drunk. I looked at the others. A second before they'd been laughing and talking, but now there was only the sound of the record player. I think Tahir understood. I looked at Alan. He had a look on his face like a dog that's been whipped. The others were looking at him too.

'I don't want any,' he said.

Mr Hadley, his red face shining still with the sweat of the game, came in and said that it had been damned hard selection and if we put in a bit of practice we could beat the Atlases. 'Fine cricket,' he said, and he rubbed his hands as usual. 'With fine weather it'll be finer.'

Tahir was silent on the way home. He kept looking at his feet as we walked, and he looked thinner and even smaller than he normally looked.

When I got home, Mrs Biggles was there in the kitchen. 'They suspect typhus, the girl's shaking with fever and the poor dear didn't even recognise her own mother,' she was saying. She was asking Lynn questions about the girl Jenny who was in hospital. 'It's not known here,' the doctor said to her mother, 'it's the foreigners have brought it in, that's for sure, from Istanbul and Pakistan and now from that Ugandan Asians' place. We've never had these things here,' he went on.

'It's the blacks bring these things in here . . .' she said.

My mum went dead silent. After Mrs Biggles had left, my dad put his mug of tea on the table and said he didn't want Mrs Biggles and her filthy mouth in his house, but Mum pretended she didn't hear and kept looking at the telly screen.

Another odd thing happened, on the following Monday. I woke up and dressed for school. Usually by the time my cornflakes are on the table, Dad's gone to work, but I found him in the kitchen that morning. He looked worried. He was sitting at the kitchen table with his hair brushed back and shiny with hair oil. He was talking to Mum, and then he took his coat and left. Mum said the people on the estate were rats and they needed poisoning, or leastways they deserved it. 'He took him to the pub once,' she said, 'just once as far as I know.'

'Who?' I asked.

'That Mr Habib from next door, your Tahir's father, even though the poor man couldn't drink on account of his religion, he had to drag him along just to show everyone.'

'Who took him?'

'Them people from C,' she said, 'they've painted things on our door. I wish Dad would call the police.'

As I walked out to school I turned to the door and it said 'K B W' in big black letters.

Dad was furious with Mum for telling me about it, and they had a right row that evening. Mum had scrubbed it off the door with sandpaper.

'Did you come back with Tahir?' she asked.

Tahir had been at school that day, but he behaved a bit strange. He wasn't there for the last lesson and I reckoned he must have hopped it.

'What does it mean?' I asked my dad, remembering the letters.
'It means your dad is poking his nose into other people's business,' my mum said.

'I saw it,' I said.

'It means Keep Britain White,' Dad said. He looked grey in the face and serious. 'You know what that means, son. It used to be the Jews in the thirties, now it's bleedin' Indians and Pakistanis. Some people have seen you with Tahir.'

'More like they've seen you chatting like old friends to Habash, or whatever his name is,' Mum said.

'I've seen a lot of it and hoped you wouldn't grow up in a world with these anti-working-class prejudices. I don't care what your mum says, but we've got to fight it. I've been fighting it, and I hope my son and grandson will fight it too.'

'And a lot of good it's done you,' Mum said.

But I was kind of proud of my dad.

'They are fascist scum, lad,' he said. He always calls me 'lad' when he gets to lecturing about his politics.

'Don't go putting your ideas into the boy's head, you leave him to think as he pleases.'

Dad ignored her. He sat with his palms on his knees and with his tall back pushed against the chair, the way he always did when he thought he was teaching me the facts of life.

'You know this typhoid, lad,' he said. 'People are blaming the Habibs for bringing it in. But any law court in this country knows they're innocent. It's ignorance and superstition. This girl Jenny went to Spain on the school trip with our Lynn, didn't she?' This was said more to Mum than to me.

I hardly slept at all that night. The next day the papers said that the girl Jenny was worse and that several cases of typhoid had been found and more people had been put under observation in the East End hospitals. I was thinking that I knew why the cricket team hadn't wanted to touch Tahir's cocoa. I was wishing I had picked it up. I knew that Tahir must be thinking the same thing too. It struck me that he must have thought that I had the same idea as the rest of them.

Sometimes I have funny dreams and that's when I can't sleep. That night I dreamt of the letters K B W painted up across our door, and then the letters spread out with other letters on to the whole of the estate, and the letters growing and becoming bigger and bigger till they were too heavy and had to come crashing down, falling on top of me, the K like two great legs and the W spinning round like giant compasses.

I went very tired to school. I didn't tell Mum about the dream. Tahir wasn't in the playground and he wasn't at registration. I thought he might be late, but he never came late, and then it struck me that I knew he wouldn't come to school that day.

I stayed in that night and so did Dad. He usually goes down the pub for a jar, but he didn't bother that night. He turned on the telly and I could see from the way he folded his legs, and from his eyes which were glued on the screen but not taking in the programme, that he was worried. He usually starts on at Lynn when he's like that, asks her to polish her shoes for school the next day and for her homework and everything. It felt to me too as though something was about to happen, and it did.

I heard the crash and then another thud and another crash of glass and a woman screaming. It was Tahir's mother. Dad sprang up from his chair. I felt that he had been expecting it. He rushed to the door. Mum came out of the kitchen. The crash of brick or stone sounded as though it was in our own house. Dad opened the door and went out on to the gallery.

'Bastard, cowards!' I heard. It was Mr Habib shouting his lungs out.

Dad rushed back into the flat. 'There's twenty of them out there.'

'Shall I call the police?' Mum asked.

Dad didn't answer. Everyone hates coppers on our estate, and no one ever calls them. Coppers don't need invitations. I could hear the blokes downstairs shouting. Mum pushed Lynn away from her and went out on to the gallery.

Mr Habib was still shouting, 'You are all bastards, white bastards'.

Then we heard the running steps on the stairs. The blokes were coming up, and they were shouting too: 'Paki filth,' and, 'The girl's dead'.

It was all hell. Mr Habib went in and got Tahir's cricket bat. The blokes from C Block had bottles. There was more crashing of glass and Mrs Habib kept screaming things in Indian and I could hear Tahir crying and shouting and a lot of thumping.

'Why don't you help him?' my mum shouted to Dad. 'What kind of bloody Communist are you?' But Dad was pushing her into the kitchen.

'Shut your mouth,' he said to her. He never talks like that normally, but he looked as though he'd pissed himself. 'Let the police handle this. There's twenty of them out there.'

By the time the police came, the sirens blaring, pulling into the courtyard, jumping out and slamming their car doors, the blokes were gone.

I said, 'Mum I'm going out,' and before she could stop me I went to the door and unbolted it. Other people had come out of their flats. The galleries of all the floors were now full of people trying to see what had happened. The police called an ambulance, and they took Mr Habib, who was lying outside his door groaning, to hospital. Tahir was bending over him when the coppers came with an Indian bloke and started asking question. Tahir looked up at me as I stepped out, and he looked away. His dad had all blood streaming down his face. The day after, the blood marks were still there, all over the gallery.

Two hours later, we were all still awake. It was still as death outside and silent.

'I'll take it up with the council,' my dad said. I knew what he felt. He had wanted to help Tahir's dad, I am sure, but he felt helpless. There were too many of the others, he couldn't have said nothing.

'I wouldn't be seen dead at that girl's funeral,' Dad said after a while.

Four Indian blokes came and took Tahir and his mum and all their stuff away that same night and we could hear the coppers who'd stayed behind arguing with them.

The next day at cricket Hadley asked me where Tahir was. The other boys told him the whole story, that bricks had been thrown through their windows and that Tahir's dad was in hospital.

Mr Hadley knew our school and he turned up there the next day. The Headmaster sent for Tahir and for me from class and we walked together to the office without a word. Mr Hadley was there. He said he was sorry to hear that Tahir's family had been in an unfortunate incident and that he wanted Tahir to come to cricket practice.

Tahir answered all his questions about where they were living and that. He said, 'Yes, sir,' when Mr Hadley said that he must realise that he had a lot of good friends like me and that wherever he lived he must continue to play for Devonmount. He said, 'Yes, sir,' his legs apart, his hands folded behind his back, his head bent and his lips tight together, his eyes moving from Mr Hadley's face to the floor. But he never came again.

Nineteen Fifty-Five

Alice Walker

1955

The car is a brandnew red Thunderbird convertible, and it's passed the house more than once. It slows down real slow now, and stops at the curb. An older gentleman dressed like a Baptist deacon gets out on the side near the house, and a young fellow who looks about sixteen gets out on the driver's side. They are white, and I wonder what in the world they doing in this neighborhood.

Well, I say to J. T., put your shirt on, anyway, and let me clean these glasses offa the table.

We had been watching the ballgame on TV. I wasn't actually watching, I was sort of daydreaming, with my foots up in J. T.'s lap.

I seen 'em coming on up the walk, brisk, like they coming to sell something, and then they rung the bell, and J. T. declined to put on a shirt but instead disappeared into the bedroom where the other television is. I turned down the one in the living room; I figured I'd be rid of these two double quick and J. T. could come back out again.

Are you Gracie Mae Still? asked the old guy, when I opened the door and put my hand on the lock inside the screen.

And I don't need to buy a thing, said I.

What makes you think we're sellin'? he asks, in that hearty Southern way that makes my eyeballs ache.

Well, one way or another and they're inside the house and the first thing the young fellow does is raise the TV a couple of decibels. He's about five feet nine, sort of womanish looking, with real dark white skin and a red pouting mouth. His hair is black and curly and he looks like a Loosianna creole.

About one of your songs, says the deacon. He is maybe sixty, with white hair and beard, white silk shirt, black linen suit, black tie and black shoes. His cold gray eyes look like they're sweating.

One of my songs?

Traynor here just *loves* your songs. Don't you, Traynor? He nudges Traynor with his elbow. Traynor blinks, says something I can't catch in a pitch I don't register.

The boy learned to sing and dance livin' round you people out in the country. Practically cut his teeth on you.

Traynor looks up at me and bites his thumbnail.

I laugh.

Well, one way or another they leave with my agreement that they can record one of my songs. The deacon writes me a check for five hundred dollars, the boy grunts his awareness of the transaction, and I am laughing all over myself by the time I rejoin J. T.

Just as I am snuggling down beside him though I hear the front door bell going off again.

Forgit his hat? asks J. T.

I hope not, I say.

The deacon stands there leaning on the door frame and once again I'm thinking of those sweaty-looking eyeballs of his. I wonder if sweat makes your eyeballs pink because his are sure pink. Pink and gray and it strikes me that nobody I'd care to know is behind them.

I forgot one little thing, he says pleasantly. I forgot to tell you Traynor and I would like to buy up all of those records you made of the song. I tell you we sure do love it.

Well, love it or not, I'm not so stupid as to let them do that without making 'em pay. So I says, Well, that's gonna cost you. Because, really, that song never did sell all that good, so I was glad they was going to buy it up. But on the other hand, them two listening to my song by themselves, and nobody else getting to hear me sing it, give me a pause.

Well, one way or another the deacon showed me where I would come out ahead on any deal he had proposed so far. Didn't I give you five hundred dollars? he asked. What white man – and don't even need to mention colored – would give you more? We buy up all your records of that particular song: first, you git royalties. Let me ask you, how much you sell that song for in the first place? Fifty dollars? A hundred, I say. And no royalties from it yet, right? Right. Well, when we buy up all of them records you gonna git royalties. And that's gonna make all them race record shops sit up and take notice of Gracie Mae Still. And they gonna push all them other records of yourn they got. And you no doubt will become one of the big name colored recording artists. And then we can offer you another five hundred dollars for letting us do all this for you. And by God you'll be sittin' pretty! You can go out and buy you the kind of outfit a star should have. Plenty sequins and yards of red satin.

I had done unlocked the screen when I saw I could get some more money out of him. Now I held it wide open while he squeezed through the opening between me and the door. He whipped out another piece of paper and I signed it.

He sort of trotted out to the car and slid in beside Traynor, whose head was back against the seat. They swung around in a u-turn in front of the house and then they was gone.

J. T. was putting his shirt on when I got back to the bedroom. Yankees beat the Orioles 10–6, he said. I believe I'll drive out to Paschal's pond and go fishing. Wanta go?

While I was putting on my pants J. T. was holding the two checks.

I'm real proud of a woman that can make cash money without leavin' home, he said. And I said *Umph*. Because we met on the road with me singing in first one little low-life jook after another, making ten dollars a night for myself if I was lucky, and sometimes bringin' home nothing but my life. And J. T. just loved them times. The way I was fast and flashy and always on the go from one town to another. He loved the way my singin' made the dirt farmers cry like babies and the womens shout Honey, hush! But that's mens. They loves any style to which you can get 'em accustomed.

1956

My little grandbaby called me one night on the phone: Little Mama, Little Mama, there's a white man on the television singing one of your songs! Turn on channel 5.

Lord, if it wasn't Traynor. Still looking half asleep from the neck up, but kind of awake in a nasty way from the waist down. He wasn't doing too bad with my song either, but it wasn't just the song the people in the audience was screeching and screaming over, it was that nasty little jerk he was doing from the waist down.

Well, Lord have mercy, I said, listening to him. If I'da closed my eyes, it could have been me. He had followed every turning of my voice, side streets, avenues, red lights, train crossings and all. It give me a chill.

Everywhere I went I heard Traynor singing my song, and all the little white girls just eating it up. I never had so many ponytails switched across my line of vision in my life. They was so *proud*. He was a *genius*.

Well, all that year I was trying to lose weight anyway and that and high blood pressure and sugar kept me pretty well occupied. Traynor had made a smash from a song of mine, I still had seven hundred dollars of the original one thousand dollars in the bank, and I felt if I could just bring my weight down, life would be sweet.

1957

I lost ten pounds in 1956. That's what I give myself for Christmas. And J. T. and me and the children and their friends and grandkids of all description had just finished dinner – over which I had put on nine and a half of my lost ten – when who should appear at the front door but Traynor. Little Mama, Little Mama! It's that white man who sings ——, —— ——. The children didn't call it my song anymore. Nobody did. It was funny how that happened. Traynor and the deacon had bought up all my records, true, but on his record he had put 'written by Gracie Mae Still'. But that was just another name on the label, like 'produced by Apex Records'.

On the TV he was inclined to dress like the deacon told him: But now he looked presentable.

Merry Christmas, said he.

And same to you, Son.

I don't know why I called him Son. Well, one way or another they're all our sons. The only requirement is that they be younger than us. But then again, Traynor seemed to be aging by the minute.

You looks tired, I said. Come on in and have a glass of Christmas cheer.

J. T. ain't never in his life been able to act decent to a white man he wasn't working for, but he poured Traynor a glass of bourbon and water, then he took all the children and grandkids and friends and whatnot out to the den. After while I heard Traynor's voice singing the song, coming from the stereo console. It was just the kind of Christmas present my kids would consider cute.

I looked at Traynor, complicit. But he looked like it was the last thing in the world he wanted to hear. His head was pitched forward over his lap, his hands holding his glass and his elbows on his knees.

I done sung that song seem like a million times this year, he said. I sung it on the Grand Ole Opry, I sung it on the Ed Sullivan show. I sung it on Mike Douglas, I sung it at the Cotton Bowl, the Orange Bowl. I sung it at Festivals. I sung it at Fairs. I sung it overseas in Rome, Italy, and once in a submarine *underseas*. I've sung it and sung it, and I'm making forty thousand dollars a day offa it, and you know what, I don't have the faintest notion what that song means.

Whatchumean, what do it mean? It mean what it says. All I could think was: 'These suckers is making forty thousand a *day* offa my song and now they gonna come back and try to swindle me out of the original thousand.

It's just a song, I said. Cagey. When you fool around with a lot of no count mens you sing a bunch of 'em. I shrugged.

Oh, he said. Well. He started brightening up. I just come by to tell you I think you are a great singer.

He didn't blush, saying that. Just said it straight out.

And I brought you a little Christmas present too. Now you take this little box and you hold it until I drive off. Then you take it outside under that first streetlight back up the street aways in front of that green house. Then you open the box and see . . . Well, just *see*.

What had come over this boy, I wondered, holding the box. I looked out the window in time to see another white man come up and get in the car with him and then two more cars full of white mens start out behind him. They was all in long black cars that looked like a funeral procession.

Little Mama, Little Mama, what it is? One of my grandkids came running up and started pulling at the box. It was wrapped in gay Christmas paper – the thick, rich kind that it's hard to picture folks making just to throw away.

J. T. and the rest of the crowd followed me out the house, up the street to the streetlight and in front of the green house. Nothing was there but somebody's goldgrilled white Cadillac. Brandnew and most distracting. We got to looking at it so till I almost forgot the little box in my hand. While the other were busy making 'miration I carefully took off the paper and ribbon and folded them up and put them in my pants pocket. What should I see but a pair of genuine solid gold caddy keys.

Dangling the keys in front of everybody's nose, I unlocked the caddy, motioned for J. T. to git in on the other side, and us didn't come back home for two days.

1960

Well, the boy was sure nuff famous by now. He was still a mite shy of twenty but already they was calling him the Emperor of Rock and Roll.

Then what should happen but the draft.

Well, says J. T. There goes all this Emperor of Rock and Roll business.

But even in the army the womens was on him like white on rice. We watched it on the News.

Dear Gracie Mae [he wrote from Germany],

How you? Fine I hope as this leaves me doing real well. Before I come in the army I was gaining a lot of weight and gitting jittery from making all them dumb movies. But now I exercise and eat right and get plenty of rest. I'm more awake than I been in ten years.

I wonder if you are writing any more songs?

Sincerely,
Traynor

I wrote him back:

Dear Son,

We is all fine in the Lord's good grace and hope this finds you the same. J. T. and me be out all times of the day and night in that car you give me – which you know you didn't have to do. Oh, and I do appreciate the mink and the new self-cleaning oven. But if you send anymore stuff to eat from Germany I'm going to have to open up a store in the neighborhood just to get rid of it. Really, we have more than enough of everything. The Lord is good to us and we don't know Want.

Glad to here you is well and gitting your right rest. There ain't nothing like exercising to help that along. J. T. and me work some part of every day that we don't go fishing in the garden.

Well, so long Soldier.

Sincerely
Gracie Mae

He wrote:

Dear Gracie Mae,

I hope you and J. T. like that automatic power tiller I had one of the stores back home send you. I went through a mountain of catalogs looking for it – I wanted something that even a woman could use.

I've been thinking about writing some songs of my own but every time I finish one it don't seem to be about nothing I've actually lived myself. My agent keeps sending me other people's songs but they just sound mooney. I can hardly git through 'em without gagging.

Everybody still loves that song of yours. They ask me all the time what do I think it means, really. I mean, they want to know just what *I* want to know. Where out of your life did it come from?

Sincerely,
Traynor

1968

I didn't see the boy for seven years. No. Eight. Because just everybody was dead when I saw him again. Malcolm X, King, the president and his brother, and even J. T. J. T. died of a head cold. It just settled in his head like a block of ice, he said, and nothing we did moved it until one day he just leaned out the bed and died.

His good friend Horace helped me put him away, and then about a year later Horace and me started going together. We was sitting out on the front porch swing one summer night, dusk-dark, and I saw this great procession of lights winding to a stop.

Holy Toledo! said Horace. (He's got a real sexy voice like Ray Charles.) Look *at* it. He meant the long line of flashy cars and the white men in white summer suits jumping out on the drivers' sides and standing at attention. With wings they could pass for angels, with hoods they could be the Klan.

Traynor comes waddling up the walk.

And suddenly I know what it is he could pass for. An Arab like the ones you see in storybooks. Plump and soft and with never a care about weight. Because with so much money, who cares? Traynor is almost dressed like someone from a storybook too. He has on, I swear, about ten necklaces. Two sets of bracelets on his arms, at least one ring on every finger, and some kind of shining buckles on his shoes so that when he walks you get quite a few twinkling lights.

Gracie Mae, he says, coming up to give me a hug. J. T.

I explain that J. T. passed. That this is Horace.

Horace, he says, puzzled but polite, sort of rocking back on his heels, Horace.

That's it for Horace. He goes in the house and don't come back.

Looks like you and me is gained a few, I say.

He laughs. The first time I ever heard him laugh. It don't sound much like a laugh and I can't swear that it's better than no laugh a'tall.

He's gitting fat for sure, but he's still slim compared to me. I'll never see three hundred pounds again and I've just about said (excuse me) fuck it. I got to thinking about it one day an' I thought: aside from the fact that they say it's unhealthy, my fat ain't never been no trouble. Mens always have loved me. My kids ain't never complained. Plus they's fat. And fat like I is I looks distinguished. You see me coming and know somebody's *there*.

Gracie Mae, he says, I've come with a personal invitation to you to my house tomorrow for dinner. He laughed. What did it sound like? I couldn't place it. See them men out there? he asked me. I'm sick and tired of eating with them. They don't never have nothing to talk about. That's why I eat so much. But if you come to dinner tomorrow we can talk about the old days. You can tell me about that farm I bought you.

I sold it, I said.

You did?

Yeah, I said, I did. Just cause I said I liked to exercise by working in a garden didn't mean I wanted five hundred acres! Anyhow, I'm a city girl now. Raised in the country it's true. Dirt poor – the whole bit – but that's all behind me now.

Oh well, he said, I didn't mean to offend you.

We sat a few minutes listening to the crickets.

Then he said: You wrote that song while you was still on the farm, didn't you, or was it right after you left?

You had somebody spying on me? I asked.

You and Bessie Smith got into a fight over it once, he said.

You *is* been spying on me!

But I don't know what the fight was about, he said. Just like I don't know what happened to your second husband. Your first one died in the Texas electric chair. Did you know that? Your third one beat you up, stole your touring costumes and your car and retired with a chorine to Tuskege. He laughed. He's still there.

I had been mad, but suddenly I calmed down. Traynor was talking very dreamily. It was dark but seems like I could tell his eyes weren't right. It was like some*thing* was sitting there talking to me but not necessarily with a person behind it.

You gave up on marrying and seem happier for it. He laughed again. I married but it never went like it was supposed to. I never could squeeze any of my own life either into it or out of it. It was like singing somebody else's record. I copied the way it was sposed to be *exactly* but I never had a clue what marriage meant.

I bought her a diamond ring big as your fist. I bought her clothes. I built her a mansion. But right away she didn't want the boys to stay there. Said they smoked up the bottom floor. Hell, there were *five* floors.

No need to grieve, I said. No need to. Plenty more where she come from.

He perked up. That's part of what that song means, ain't it? No need to grieve. Whatever it is, there's plenty more down the line.

I never really believed that way back when I wrote that song, I said. It was all bluffing then. The trick is to live long enough to put your young bluffs to use. Now if I was to sing that song today I'd tear it up. 'Cause I done lived long enough to know it's *true*. Them words could hold me up.

I ain't lived that long, he said.

Look like you on your way, I said. I don't know why, but the boy seemed to need some encouraging. And I don't know, seem like one way or another you talk to rich white folks and you end up reassuring *them*. But what the hell, by now I feel something for the boy. I wouldn't be in his bed all alone in the middle of the night for nothing. Couldn't be nothing worse than being famous the world over for something you don't even understand. That's what I tried to tell Bessie. She wanted the same song. Overheard me practising it one day, said, with her hands on her hips: Gracie Mae, I'ma sing your song tonight. I *likes* it.

Your lips be too swole to sing, I said. She was mean and she was strong, but I trounced her.

Ain't you famous enough with your own stuff? I said. Leave mine alone. Later on, she thanked me. By then she was Miss Bessie Smith to the World, and I was still Miss Gracie Mae Nobody from Notasulga.

The next day all these limousines arrived to pick me up. Five cars and twelve bodyguards. Horace picked that morning to start painting the kitchen.

Don't paint the kitchen, fool, I said. The only reason that dumb boy of ours is going to show me his mansion is because he intends to present us with a new house.

What you gonna do with it? he asked me, standing there in his shirtsleeves stirring the paint.

Sell it. Give it to the children. Live in it on weekends. It don't matter what I do. He sure don't care.

Horace just stood there shaking his head. Mama you sure looks *good*, he says. Wake me up when you git back.

Fool, I say, and pat my wig in front of the mirror.

The boy's house is something else. First you come to this mountain, and then you commence to drive and drive up this road that's lined with magnolias. Do magnolias grow on mountains? I was wondering. And you come to lakes and you come to ponds and you come to deer and you come up on some sheep. And I figure these two is sposed to represent England and Wales. Or something out of Europe. And you just keep on coming to stuff. And it's all pretty. Only the man driving my car don't look at nothing but the road. Fool. And then *finally*, after all this time, you begin to go up the driveway. And there's more magnolias – only they're not in such good shape. It's sort of cool up this high and I don't think they're gonna make it. And then I see this building that looks like if it had a name it would be The Tara Hotel. Columns and steps and outdoor chandeliers and rocking chairs. Rocking chairs? Well, and there's the boy on the steps dressed in a dark green satin jacket like you see folks wearing on TV late at night, and he looks sort of like a fat dracula with all that house rising behind him, and standing beside him there's this little white vision of loveliness that he introduces as his wife.

He's nervous when he introduces us and he says to her: This is Gracie Mae Still, I want you to know me. I mean . . . and she give him a look that would fry meat.

Won't you come in, Gracie Mae, she says, and that's the last I see of her.

He fishes around for something to say or do and decides to escort me to the kitchen. We go through the entry and the parlor and the breakfast room and the dining room and the servants' passage and finally get there. The first thing I notice is that, altogether, there are five stoves. He looks about to introduce me to one.

Wait a minute, I say. Kitchens don't do nothing for me. Let's go sit on the front porch.

Well, we hike back and we sit in the rocking chairs rocking until dinner.

Gracie Mae, he says down the table, taking a piece of fried chicken from the woman standing over him, I got a little surprise for you.

It's a house, ain't it? I ask, spearing a chitlin.

You're getting *spoiled*, he says. And the ways he says *spoiled* sounds funny. He slurs it. It sounds like his tongue is too thick for his mouth. Just that quick he's finished the chicken and is now eating chitlins *and* a pork chop. *Me* spoiled, I'm thinking.

I already got a house. Horace is right this minute painting the kitchen. I bought that house. My kids feel comfortable in that house.

But this one I bought you is just like mine. Only a little smaller.

I still don't need no house. And anyway who would clean it?

He looks surprised.

Really, I think, some peoples advance *so* slowly.

I hadn't thought of that. But what the hell, I'll get you somebody to live in.

I don't want other folks living 'round me. Makes me nervous.

You *don't*? It *do*?

What I want to wake up and see folks I don't even know for?

He just sits there downtable staring at me. Some of that feeling is in the song, ain't it? Not the words, the *feeling*. What I want to wake up and see folks I don't even know for? But I see twenty folks a day I don't even know, including my wife.

This food wouldn't be bad to wake up to though, I said. The boy had found the genius of corn bread.

He looked at me real hard. He laughed. Short. They want what you got but they don't want you. They want what I got only it ain't mine. That's what makes 'em so hungry for me when I sing. They getting the flavor of something but they ain't getting the thing itself. They like a pack of hound dogs trying to gobble up a scent.

You talking 'bout your fans?

Right. Right. He says.

Don't worry 'bout your fans, I say. They don't know their asses from a hole in the ground. I doubt there's a honest one in the bunch.

That's the point. Dammit, that's the point! He hits the table with his fist. It's so solid it don't even quiver. You need a honest audience! You can't have folks that's just gonna lie right back to you.

Yea, I say, it was small compared to yours, but I had one. It would have been worth my life to try to sing 'em somebody else's stuff that I didn't know nothing about.

He must have pressed a buzzer under the table. One of his flunkies zombies up.

Git Johnny Carson, he says.

On the phone? asks the zombie.

On the phone, says Traynor, what you think I mean, git him offa the front porch? Move your ass.

So two weeks later we's on the Johnny Carson show.

Traynor is all corseted down nice and looks a little bit fat but mostly good. And all the women that grew up on him and my song squeal and squeal. Traynor says: The lady who wrote my first hit record is here with us tonight, and she's agreed to sing it for all of us, just like she sung it forty-five years ago. Ladies and Gentlemen, the great Gracie Mae Still!

Well, I had tried to lose a couple of pounds my own self, but failing that I had me a very big dress made. So I sort of rolls over next to Traynor, who is dwarfted by me, so that when he puts his arm around back of me to try to hug me it looks funny to the audience and they laugh.

I can see this pisses him off. But I smile out there at 'em. Imagine squealing for twenty years and not knowing why you're squealing? No more sense of endings and beginnings than hogs.

It don't matter, Son, I say. Don't fret none over me.

I commence to sing. And I sound —— wonderful. Being able to sing good ain't all about having a good singing voice a'tall. A good singing voice helps. But when you come up in the Hard Shell Baptist church like I did you understand early that the fellow that sings is the singer. Them that waits for programs and arrangements and letters from home is just good voices occupying body space.

So there I am singing my own song, my own way. And I give it all I got and enjoy every minute of it. When I finish Traynor is standing up clapping and clapping and beaming at first me and then the audience like I'm his mama for true. The audience claps politely for about two seconds.

Traynor looks disgusted.

He comes over and tries to hug me again. The audience laughs.

Johnny Carson looks at us like we both weird.

Traynor is mad as hell. He's supposed to sing something called a love ballad. But instead he takes the mike, turns to me and says: Now see if my imitation still holds up. He goes into the same song, *our* song, I think, looking out at his flaky audience. And he sings it just the way he always did. My voice, my tone, my inflection, everything. But he forgets a couple of lines. Even before he's finished the matronly squeals begin.

He sits down next to me looking whipped.

It don't matter, Son, I say, patting his hand. You don't even know those people. Try to make the people you know happy.

Is that in the song? he asks.

Maybe. I say.

1977

For a few years I hear from him, then nothing. But trying to lose weight takes all the attention I got to spare. I finally faced up to the fact that my fat is the hurt I don't admit, not even to myself, and that I been trying to bury it from the day I was born. But also when you git real old, to tell the truth, it ain't as pleasant. It gits lumpy and slack. Yuck. So one day I said to Horace, I'ma git this shit offa me.

And he fell in with the program like he always try to do and Lord such a procession of salads and cottage cheese and fruit juice.

One night I dreamed Traynor had split up with his fifteenth wife. He said: You meet 'em for no reason. You date 'em for no reason. You marry 'em for no reason. I do it all but I swear it's just like somebody else doing it. I feel like I can't remember Life.

The boy's in trouble, I said to Horace.

You've always said that, he said.

I have?

Yeah. You always said he looked asleep. You can't sleep through life if you wants to live it.

You not such a fool after all, I said, pushing myself up with my cane and hobbling over to where he was. Let me sit down on your lap, I said, while this salad I ate takes effect.

In the morning we heard Traynor was dead. Some said fat, some said heart, some said alcohol, some said drugs. One of the children called from Detroit. Them dumb fans of his is on a crying rampage, she said. You just ought to turn on the TV.

But I didn't want to see 'em. They was crying and crying and didn't even know what they was crying for. One day this is going to be a pitiful country, I thought.

Country Lovers

Nadine Gordimer

The farm children play together when they are small; but once the white children go away to school they soon don't play together any more, even in the holidays. Although most of the black children get some sort of schooling, they drop every year farther behind the grades passed by the white children; the childish vocabulary, the child's exploration of the adventurous possibilities of dam, koppies, mealie lands and veld – there comes a time when the white children have surpassed these with the vocabulary of boarding-school and the possibilities of inter-school sports matches and the kind of adventures seen at the cinema. This usefully coincides with the age of twelve or thirteen; so that by the time early adolescence is reached, the black children are making, along with the bodily changes common to all, an easy transition to adult forms of address, beginning to call their old playmates *missus* and *baasie* – little master.

The trouble was Paulus Eysendyck did not seem to realize that Thebedi was now simply one of the crowd of farm children down at the kraal, recognizable in his sisters' old clothes. The first Christmas holidays after he had gone to boarding-school he brought home for Thebedi a painted box he had made in his wood-work class. He had to give it to her secretly because he had nothing for the other children at the kraal. And she gave him, before he went back to school, a bracelet she had made of thin brass wire and the grey-and-white beans of the castor-oil crop his father cultivated. (When they used to play together, she was the one who had taught Paulus how to make clay oxen for their toy spans.) There was a craze, even in the *platteland* towns like the one where he was at school, for boys to wear elephant-hair and other bracelets beside their watch-straps; his was admired, friends asked him to get similar ones for them. He said the natives made them on his father's farm and he would try.

When he was fifteen, six feet tall, and tramping round at school dances with the girls from the 'sister' school in the same town; when he had learnt how to tease and flirt and fondle quite intimately these girls who were the daughters of prosperous farmers like his father; when he had even met one who, at a wedding he had attended with his parents on a nearby farm, had let him do with her in a locked storeroom what people did when they made love – when he was as far from his childhood as all this, he still brought home from a shop in town a red plastic belt and gilt hoop ear-rings for the black girl, Thebedi. She told her father the missus had given these to her as a reward for some work she had done – it was true she sometimes was called to help out in the farmhouse. She told the girls in the kraal that she had a sweetheart nobody knew about, far away, away on another farm, and they giggled, and teased, and admired her. There was a boy in the kraal called Njabulo who said he wished he could have bought her a belt and ear-rings.

When the farmer's son was home for the holidays she wandered far from the kraal and her companions. He went for walks alone. They had not arranged this; it was an urge each followed independently. He knew it was she, from a long way off. She knew that his dog would not bark at her. Down at the dried-up river-bed where five or six years ago the children had caught a leguaan one great day – a creature that combined ideally the size and ferocious aspect of the crocodile with the harmlessness of the lizard – they squatted side by side on the earth bank. He told her traveller's tales: about school, about the punishments at school, particularly, exaggerating both their nature and his indifference to them. He told her about the town of Middleburg, which she had never seen. She had nothing to tell but she prompted with many questions, like any good listener. While he talked he twisted and tugged at the roots of white stinkwood and Cape willow trees that looped out of the eroded earth around them. It had always been a good spot for children's games, down there hidden by the mesh of old, ant-eaten trees held in place by vigorous ones, wild asparagus bushing up between the trunks, and here and there prickly-pear cactus sunken-skinned and bristly, like an old man's face, keeping alive sapless until the next rainy season. She punctured the dry hide of a prickly-pear again and again with a sharp stick while she listened. She laughed a lot at what he told her, sometimes dropping her face on her knees, sharing amusement with the cool shady earth beneath her bare feet. She put on her pair of shoes – white sandals, thickly Blanco-ed against the farm dust – when he was on the farm, but these were taken off and laid aside, at the river-bed.

One summer afternoon when there was water flowing there and it was very hot she waded in as they used to do when they were children, her dress bunched modestly and tucked into the legs of her pants. The schoolgirls he went swimming with at dams or pools on neighbouring farms wore bikinis but the sight of their dazzling bellies and thighs in the sunlight had never made him feel what he felt now, when the girl came up the bank and sat beside him, the drops of water beading off her dark legs the only points of light in the earth-smelling, deep shade. They were not afraid of one another, they had known one another always; he did with her what he had done that time in the storeroom at the wedding, and this time it was so lovely, so lovely, he was surprised . . . and she was surprised by it, too – he could see in her dark face that was part of the shade, with her big dark eyes, shiny as soft water, watching him attentively: as she had when they used to huddle over their teams of mud oxen, as she had when he told her about detention weekends at school.

They went to the river-bed often through those summer holidays. They met just before the light went, as it does quite quickly, and each returned home with the dark – she to her mother's hut, he to the farmhouse – in time for the evening meal. He did not tell her about school or town any more. She did not ask questions any longer. He told her, each time, when they would meet again. Once or twice it was very early in the morning; the lowing of the cows being driven to graze came to them where they lay, dividing them with unspoken recognition of the sound read in their two pairs of eyes, opening so close to each other.

He was a popular boy at school. He was in the second, then the first soccer team. The head girl of the 'sister' school was said to have a crush on him; he didn't particularly like her, but there was a pretty blonde who put up her long hair into a kind of doughnut with a black ribbon round it, whom he took to see films when the schoolboys and girls had a free Saturday afternoon. He had been driving tractors and other farm vehicles since he was ten years old, and as soon as he was eighteen he got a driver's licence and in the holidays, this last year of his school life, he took neighbours' daughters to dances and to the drive-in cinema that had just opened twenty kilometres from the farm. His sisters were married, by then; his parents often left him in charge of the farm over the weekend while they visited the young wives and grandchildren.

When Thebedi saw the farmer and his wife drive away on a Saturday afternoon, the boot of their Mercedes filled with fresh-killed poultry and vegetables from the garden that it was part of her father's work to tend, she knew that she must come not to the river-bed but up to the house. The house was an old one, thick-walled, dark against the heat. The kitchen was its lively thoroughfare, with servants, food supplies, begging cats and dogs, pots boiling over, washing being damped for ironing, and the big deep-freeze the missus had ordered from town, bearing a crocheted mat and a vase of plastic irises. But the dining-room with the bulging-legged heavy table was shut up in its rich, old smell of soup and tomato sauce. The sitting-room curtains were drawn and the TV set silent. The door of the parents' bedroom was locked and the empty rooms where the girls had slept had sheets of plastic spread over the beds. It was in one of these that she and the farmer's son stayed together whole nights – almost: she had to get away before the house servants, who knew her, came in at dawn. There was a risk someone would discover her or traces of her presence if he took her to his own bedroom, although she had looked into it many times when she was helping out in the house and knew well, there, the row of silver cups he had won at school.

When she was eighteen and the farmer's son nineteen and working with his father on the farm before entering a veterinary college, the young man Njabulo asked her father for her. Njabulo's parents met with hers and the money he was to pay in place of the cows it is customary to give a prospective bride's parents was settled upon. He had no cows to offer; he was a labourer on the Eysendyck farm, like her father. A bright youngster; old Eysendyck had taught him brick-laying and was using him for odd jobs in construction, around the place. She did not tell the farmer's son that her parents had arranged for her to marry. She did not tell him, either, before he left for his first term at the veterinary college, that she thought she was going to have a baby. Two months after her marriage to Njabulo, she gave birth to a daughter. There was no disgrace in that; among her people it is customary for a young man to make sure, before marriage, that the chosen girl is not barren, and Njabulo had made love to her then. But the infant was very light and did not quickly grow darker as most African babies do. Already at birth there was on its head a quantity of straight, fine floss, like that which carries the seeds of certain weeds in the veld. The unfocused eyes it opened were grey flecked with yellow. Njabulo was the matt, opaque coffee-grounds colour that has always been called black; the colour of Thebedi's legs on which beaded water looked oyster-shell blue, the same colour as Thebedi's face, where the black eyes, with their interested gaze and clear whites, were so dominant.

Njabulo made no complaint. Out of his farm labourer's earnings he bought from the Indian store a cellophane-windowed pack containing a pink plastic bath, six napkins, a card of safety pins, a knitted jacket, cap and bootees, a dress, and a tin of Johnson's Baby Powder, for Thebedi's baby.

When it was two weeks old Paulus Eysendyck arrived home from the veterinary college for the holidays. He drank a glass of fresh, still-warm milk in the childhood familiarity of his mother's kitchen and heard her discussing with the old house-servant where they could get a reliable substitute to help out now that the girl Thebedi had had a baby. For the first time since he was a boy he came right into the kraal. It was eleven o'clock in the morning. The men were at work in the lands. He looked about him, urgently; the women turned away, each not wanting to be the one approached to point out where Thebedi lived. Thebedi appeared, coming slowly from the hut Njabulo had built in white-man's style, with a tin chimney, and a proper window with glass panes set in straight as walls made of unfired bricks would allow. She greeted him with hands brought together and a token movement representing the respectful bob with which she was accustomed to acknowledge she was in the presence of his father or mother. He lowered his head under the doorway of her home and went in. He said, 'I want to see. Show me.'

She had taken the bundle off her back before she came out into the light to face him. She moved between the iron bedstead made up with Njabulo's checked blankets and the small wooden table where the pink plastic bath stood among food and kitchen pots, and picked up the bundle from the snugly-blanketed grocer's box where it lay. The infant was asleep; she revealed the closed, pale, plump tiny face, with a bubble of spit at the corner of the mouth, the spidery pink hands stirring. She took off the woollen cap and the straight fine hair flew up after it in static electricity, showing gilded strands here and there. He said nothing. She was watching him as she had done when they were little, and the gang of children had trodden down a crop in their games or transgressed in some other way for which he, as the farmer's son, the white one among them, must intercede with the farmer. She disturbed the sleeping face by scratching or tickling gently at a cheek with one finger, and slowly the eyes opened, saw nothing, were still asleep, and then, awake, no longer narrowed, looked out at them, grey with yellowish flecks, his own hazel eyes.

He struggled for a moment with a grimace of tears, anger and self-pity. She could not put out her hand to him. He said, 'You haven't been near the house with it?'

She shook her head.

'Never?'

Again she shook her head.

'Don't take it out. Stay inside. Can't you take it away somewhere. You must give it to someone—'

She moved to the door with him.

He said, 'I'll see what I will do. I don't know.' And then he said: 'I feel like killing myself.'

Her eyes began to glow, to thicken with tears. For a moment there was the feeling between them that used to come when they were alone down at the river-bed.

He walked out.

Two days later, when his mother and father had left the farm for the day, he appeared again. The women were away on the lands, weeding, as they were employed to do as casual labour in summer; only the very old remained, propped up on the ground outside the huts in the flies and the sun. Thebedi did not ask him in. The child had not been well; it had diarrhoea. He asked where its food was. She said, 'The milk comes from me.' He went into Njabulo's house, where the child lay; she did not follow but stayed outside the door and watched without seeing an old crone who had lost her mind, talking to herself, talking to the fowls who ignored her.

She thought she heard small grunts from the hut, the kind of infant grunt that indicates a full stomach, a deep sleep. After a time, long or short she did not know, he came out and walked away with plodding stride (his father's gait) out of sight, towards his father's house.

The baby was not fed during the night and although she kept telling Njabulo it was sleeping, he saw for himself in the morning that it was dead. He comforted her with words and caresses. She did not cry but simply sat, staring at the door. Her hands were cold as dead chickens' feet to his touch.

Njabulo buried the little baby where farm workers were buried, in the place in the veld the farmer had given them. Some of the mounds had been left to weather away unmarked, others were covered with stones and a few had fallen wooden crosses. He was going to make a cross but before it was finished the police came and dug up the grave and took away the dead baby: someone – one of the other labourers? their women? – had reported that the baby was almost white, that, strong and healthy, it had died suddenly after a visit by the farmer's son. Pathological tests on the infant corpse showed intestinal damage not always consistent with death by natural causes.

Thebedi went for the first time to the country town where Paulus had been to school, to give evidence at the preparatory examination into the charge of murder brought against him. She cried hysterically in the witness box, saying yes, yes (the gilt hoop ear-rings swung in her ears), she saw the accused pouring liquid into the baby's mouth. She said he had threatened to shoot her if she told anyone.

More than a year went by before, in the same town, the case was brought to trial. She came to Court with a new-born baby on her back. She wore gilt hoop ear-rings; she was calm; she said she had not seen what the white man did in the house.

Paulus Eysendyck said he had visited the hut but had not poisoned the child.

The Defence did not contest that there had been a love relationship between the accused and the girl, or that intercourse had taken place, but submitted there was no proof that the child was the accused's.

The judge told the accused there was strong suspicion against him but not enough proof that he had committed the crime. The Court could not accept the girl's evidence because it was clear she had committed perjury either at this trial or at the preparatory examination. There was a suggestion in the mind of the Court that she might be an accomplice in the crime; but, again, insufficient proof.

The judge commended the honourable behaviour of the husband (sitting in court in a brown-and-yellow-quartered golf cap bought for Sundays) who had not rejected his wife and had 'even provided clothes for the unfortunate infant out of his slender means'.

The verdict on the accused was 'not guilty'.

The young white man refused to accept the congratulations of press and public and left the Court with his mother's raincoat shielding his face from photographers. His father said to the press, 'I will try and carry on as best I can to hold up my head in the district.'

Interviewed by the Sunday papers, who spelled her name in a variety of ways, the black girl, speaking in her own language, was quoted beneath her photograph: 'It was a thing of our childhood, we don't see each other any more.'

Civil Peace

Chinua Achebe

Jonathan Iwegbu counted himself extraordinarily lucky. 'Happy survival!' meant so much more to him than just a current fashion of greeting old friends in the first hazy days of peace. It went deep to his heart. He had come out of the war with five inestimable blessings – his head, his wife Maria's head and the heads of three out of their four children. As a bonus he also had his old bicycle – a miracle too but naturally not to be compared to the safety of five human heads.

The bicycle had a little history of its own. One day at the height of the war it was commandeered 'for urgent military action'. Hard as its loss would have been to him he would still have let it go without a thought had he not had some doubts about the genuineness of the officer. It wasn't his disreputable rags, nor the toes peeping out of one blue and one brown canvas shoes, nor yet the two stars of his rank done obviously in a hurry in biro, that troubled Jonathan; many good and heroic soldiers looked the same or worse. It was rather a certain lack of grip and firmness in his manner. So Jonathan, suspecting he might be amenable to influence, rummaged in his raffia bag and produced the two pounds with which he had been going to buy firewood which his wife, Maria, retailed to camp officials for extra stock-fish and corn meal, and got his bicycle back. That night he buried it in the little clearing in the bush where the dead of the camp, including his own youngest son, was buried. When he dug it up again a year later after the surrender all it needed was a little palm-oil greasing. 'Nothing puzzles God,' he said in wonder.

He put it to immediate use as a taxi and accumulated a small pile of Biafran money ferrying camp officials and their families across the four-mile stretch to the nearest tarred road. His standard charge per trip was six pounds and those who had the money were only glad to be rid of some of it in this way. At the end of a fortnight he had made a small fortune of one hundred and fifteen pounds.

Then he made the journey to Enugu and found another miracle waiting for him. It was unbelievable. He rubbed his eyes and looked again and it was still standing there before him. But, needless to say, even that monumental blessing must be accounted also totally inferior to the five heads in the family. This newest miracle was his little house in Ogui Overside. Indeed nothing puzzles God! Only two houses away a huge concrete edifice some wealthy contractor had put up just before the war was a mountain of rubble. And here was Jonathan's little zinc house of no regrets built with mud blocks quite intact! Of course the doors and windows were missing and five sheets off the roof. But what was that? And anyhow he had returned to Enugu early enough to pick up bits of old zinc and wood and soggy sheets of cardboard lying around the neighbourhood before thousands more came out of their forest holes looking for the same things. He got a destitute carpenter with one old hammer, a blunt plane and a few bent and rusty nails in his tool bag to turn this assortment of wood, paper and metal into door and window shutters for five Nigerian shillings or fifty Biafran pounds. He paid the pounds, and moved in with his overjoyed family carrying five heads on their shoulders.

His children picked mangoes near the military cemetery and sold them to soldier's wives for a few pennies – real pennies this time – and his wife started making breakfast akara balls for neighbours in a hurry to start life again. With his family earnings he took his bicycle to the villages around and bought fresh palm-wine which he mixed generously in his rooms with the water which had recently started running again in the public tap down the road, and opened up a bar for soldiers and other lucky people with good money.

At first he went daily, then every other day and finally once a week, to the offices of Coal Corporation where he used to be a miner, to find out what was what. The only thing he did find in the end was that that little house of his was even a greater blessing than he had thought. Some of his fellow ex-miners who had nowhere to return at the end of the day's waiting just slept outside the doors of the offices and cooked what meal they could scrounge together in Bournvita tins. As the weeks lengthened and still nobody could say what was what Jonathan discontinued his weekly visits altogether and faced his palm-wine bar.

But nothing puzzles God. Came the day of the windfall when

after five days of endless scuffles in queues and counter-queues in the sun outside the Treasury he had twenty pounds counted into his palms as ex-gratia award for the rebel money he had turned in. It was like Christmas for him and for many others like him when the payments began. They called it (since few could manage its proper official name) *egg-rasher.*

As soon as the pound notes were placed in his palm Jonathan simply closed it tight over them and buried fist and money inside his trouser pocket. He had to be extra careful because he had seen a man a couple of days earlier collapse into near-madness in an instant before that oceanic crowd because no sooner had he got his twenty pounds than some heartless ruffian picked it off him. Though it was not right that a man in such an extremity of agony should be blamed yet many in the queues that day were able to remark quietly on the victim's carelessness, especially after he pulled out the innards of his pocket and revealed a hole in it big enough to pass a thief's head. But of course he had insisted that the money had been in the other pocket, pulling it out too to show its comparative wholeness. So one had to be careful.

Jonathan soon transferred the money to his left hand and pocket so as to leave his right free for shaking hands should the need arise, though by fixing his gaze at such an elevation as to miss all approaching human faces he made sure that the need did not arise, until he got home.

He was normally a heavy sleeper but that night he heard all the neighbourhood noises die down one after another. Even the night watchman who knocked the hour on some metal somewhere in the distance had fallen silent after knocking one o'clock. That must have been the last thought in Jonathan's mind before he was finally carried away himself. He couldn't have been gone for long, though, when he was violently awakened again.

'Who is knocking?' whispered his wife lying beside him on the floor.

'I don't know,' he whispered back breathlessly.

The second time the knocking came it was so loud and imperious that the rickety old door could have fallen down.

'Who is knocking?' he asked then, his voice parched and trembling.

'Na tief-man and him people,' came the cool reply. 'Make you hopen de door.' This was followed by the heaviest knocking of all.

Maria was the first to raise the alarm, then he followed and all their children.

'*Police-o! Thieves-o! Neighbours-o! Police-o! We are lost! We are dead! Neighbours, are you asleep? Wake up! Police-o!*'

This went on for a long time and then stopped suddenly. Perhaps they had scared the thief away. There was total silence. But only for a short while.

'You done finish?' asked the voice outside. 'Make we help you small. Oya, everybody!'

'*Police-o! Tief-man-o! Neighbours-o! we done loss-o! Police-o! . . .*'

There were at least five other voices besides the leader's.

Jonathan and his family were now completely paralysed by terror. Maria and the children sobbed inaudibly like lost souls. Jonathan groaned continuously.

The silence that followed the thieves' alarm vibrated horribly. Jonathan all but begged their leader to speak again and be done with it.

'My frien,' said he at long last, 'we don try our best for call dem but I tink say dem all done sleep-o . . . So wetin we go do now? Sometaim you wan call soja? Or you wan make we call dem for you? Soja better pass police. No be so?'

'Na so!' replied his men. Jonathan thought he heard even more voices now than before and groaned heavily. His legs were sagging under him and his throat felt like sand-paper.

'My frien, why you no de talk again. I de ask you say you wan make we call soja?'

'No'.

'Awrighto. Now make we talk business. We no be bad tief. We no like for make trouble. Trouble done finish. War done finish and all the katakata wey de for inside. No Civil War again. This time na Civil Peace. No be so?'

'Na so!' answered the horrible chorus.

'What do you want from me? I am a poor man. Everything I had went with this war. Why do you come to me? You know people who have money. We . . .'

'Awright! We know say you no get plenty money. But we sef no get even anini. So derefore make you open dis window and give us one hundred pound and we go commot. Orderwise we de come from inside now to show you guitar-boy like dis . . .'

A volley of automatic fire rang through the sky. Maria and the children began to weep aloud again.

'Ah, missisi de cry again. No need for dat. We done talk say we na good tief. We just take our small money and go nwayorly. No molest. Abi we de molest?'

'At all!' sang the chorus.

'My friends,' began Jonathan hoarsely. 'I hear what you say and I thank you. If I had one hundred pounds . . .'

'Lookia my frien, no be play we come play for your house. If we make mistake and step for inside you no go like am-o. So derefore . . .'

'To God who made me; if you come inside and find one hundred pounds, take it and shoot me and shoot my wife and children. I swear to God. The only money I have in this life is this twenty-pounds *egg-rasher* they gave me today . . .'

'OK. Time de go. Make you open dis window and bring the twenty pound. We go manage am like dat.'

There were now loud murmurs of dissent among the chorus: 'Na lie de man de lie; e get plenty money . . . Make we go inside and search properly well . . . Wetin be twenty pound? . . .'

'Shurrup!' rang the leader's voice like a lone shot in the sky and silenced the murmuring at once. 'Are you dere? Bring the money quick!'

'I am coming,' said Jonathan fumbling in the darkness with the key of the small wooden box he kept by his side on the mat.

At the first sign of light as neighbours and others assembled to commiserate with him he was already strapping his five-gallon demijohn to his bicycle carrier and his wife, sweating in the open fire, was turning over akara balls in a wide clay bowl of boiling oil. In the corner his eldest son was rinsing out dregs of yesterday's palm wine from old beer bottles.

'I count it as nothing,' he told his sympathizers, his eyes on the rope he was tying. 'What is *egg-rasher*? Did I depend on it last week? Or is it greater than other things that went with the war? I say, let *egg-rasher* perish in the flames! Let it go where everything else has gone. Nothing puzzles God.'

The Drowned Giant

J G Ballard

On the morning after the storm the body of a drowned giant was washed ashore on the beach five miles to the north-west of the city. The first news of its arrival was brought by a nearby farmer and subsequently confirmed by the local newspaper reporters and the police. Despite this the majority of people, myself among them, remained sceptical, but the return of more and more eye-witnesses attesting to the vast size of the giant was finally too much for our curiosity. The library where my colleagues and I were carrying out our research was almost deserted when we set off for the coast shortly after two o'clock, and throughout the day people continued to leave their offices and shops as accounts of the giant circulated around the city.

By the time we reached the dunes above the beach a substantial crowd had gathered, and we could see the body lying in the shallow water two hundred yards away. At first the estimates of its size seemed greatly exaggerated. It was then at low tide, and almost all the giant's body was exposed, but he appeared to be a little larger than a basking shark. He lay on his back with his arms at his sides, in an attitude of repose, as if asleep on the mirror of wet sand, the reflection of his blanched skin fading as the water receded. In the clear sunlight his body glistened like the white plumage of a sea-bird.

Puzzled by this spectacle, and dissatisfied with the matter-of-fact explanations of the crowd, my friends and I stepped down from the dunes on to the shingle. Everyone seemed reluctant to approach the giant, but half an hour later two fishermen in wading boots walked out across the sand. As their diminutive figures neared the recumbent body a sudden hubbub of conversation broke out among the spectators. The two men were completely dwarfed by the giant. Although his heels were partly submerged in the sand, the feet rose to at least twice the fisherman's height, and we immediately realized that this drowned leviathan had the mass and dimensions of the largest sperm whale.

Three fishing smacks had arrived on the scene and with keels raised remained a quarter of a mile off-shore, the crews watching from the bows. Their discretion deterred the spectators on the shore from wading out across the sand. Impatiently everyone stepped down from the dunes and waited on the shingle slopes, eager for a closer view. Around the margins of the figure the sand had been washed away, forming a hollow, as if the giant had fallen out of the sky. The two fishermen were standing between the immense plinths of the feet, waving to us like tourists among the columns of some water-lapped temple on the Nile. For a moment I feared that the giant was merely asleep and might suddenly stir and clap his heels together, but his glazed eyes stared skywards, unaware of the minuscule replicas of himself between his feet.

The fishermen then began a circuit of the corpse, strolling past the long white flanks of the legs. After a pause to examine the fingers of the supine hand, they disappeared from sight between the arm and chest, then re-emerged to survey the head, shielding their eyes as they gazed up at its Grecian profile. The shallow forehead, straight high-bridged nose and curling lips reminded me of a Roman copy of Praxiteles, and the elegantly formed cartouches of the nostrils emphasized the resemblance to monumental sculpture.

Abruptly there was a shout from the crowd, and a hundred arms pointed towards the sea. With a start I saw that one of the fishermen had climbed on to the giant's chest and was now strolling about and signalling to the shore. There was a roar of surprise and triumph from the crowd, lost in a rushing avalanche of shingle as everyone surged forward across the sand.

As we approached the recumbent figure, which was lying in a pool of water the size of a field, our excited chatter fell away again, subdued by the huge physical dimensions of this moribund colossus. He was stretched out at a slight angle to the shore, his legs carried nearer the beach, and this foreshortening had disguised his true length. Despite the two fishermen standing on his abdomen, the crowd formed itself into a wide circle, groups of three of four people tentatively advancing towards the hands and feet.

My companions and I walked around the seaward side of the giant, whose hips and thorax towered above us like the hull of a stranded ship. His pearl-coloured skin, distended by immersion in salt water, masked the contours of the enormous muscles and tendons. We passed below the left knee, which was flexed slightly, threads of damp seaweed clinging to its sides. Draped loosely across the midriff, and preserving a tenuous propriety, was a shawl of heavy open-weaved material, bleached to a pale yellow by the water. A strong odour of brine came from the garment as it steamed in the sun, mingled with the sweet but potent scent of the giant's skin.

We stopped by his shoulder and gazed up at the motionless profile. The lips were parted slightly, the open eye cloudy and occluded, as if injected with some blue milky liquid, but the delicate arches of the nostrils and eyebrows invested the face with an ornate charm that belied the brutish power of the chest and shoulders.

The ear was suspended in mid-air over our heads like a sculptured doorway. As I raised my hand to touch the pendulous lobe someone appeared over the edge of the forehead and shouted down at me. Startled by this apparition, I stepped back, and then saw that a group of youths had climbed up on to the face and were jostling each other in and out of the orbits.

People were now clambering all over the giant, whose reclining arms provided a double stairway. From the palms they walked along the forearms to the elbow and then crawled over the distended belly of the biceps to the flat promenade of the pectoral muscles which covered the upper half of the smooth hairless chest. From here they climbed up on to the face, hand over hand along the lips and nose, or forayed down the abdomen to meet others who had straddled the ankles and were patrolling the twin columns of the thighs.

We continued our circuit through the crowd, and stopped to examine the outstretched right hand. A small pool of water lay in the palm, like the residue of another world, now being kicked away by the people ascending the arm. I tried to read the palm-lines that grooved the skin, searching for some clue to the giant's character, but the distension of the tissues had almost obliterated them, carrying away all trace of the giant's identity and his last tragic predicament. The huge muscles and wrist-bones of the hand seemed to deny any sensitivity to their owner, but the delicate flexion of the fingers and the well-tended nails, each cut symmetrically to within six inches of the quick, argued a certain refinement of temperament, illustrated in the Grecian features of the face, on which the townsfolk were now sitting like flies.

One youth was even standing, arms wavering at his sides, on the very tip of the nose, shouting down at his companions, but the face of the giant still retained its massive composure.

Returning to the shore, we sat down on the shingle, and watched the continuous stream of people arriving from the city. Some six or seven fishing boats had collected off-shore, and their crews waded in through the shallow water for a closer look at this enormous storm-catch. Later a party of police appeared and made a half-hearted attempt to cordon off the beach, but after walking up to the recumbent figure any such thoughts left their minds, and they went off together with bemused backward glances.

An hour later there were a thousand people present on the beach, at least two hundred of them standing or sitting on the giant, crowded along his arms and legs or circulating in a ceaseless mêlée across his chest and stomach. A large gang of youths occupied the head, toppling each other off the cheeks and sliding down the smooth planes of the jaw. Two or three straddled the nose, and another crawled into one of the nostrils, from which he emitted barking noises like a dog.

That afternoon the police returned, and cleared a way through the crowd for a party of scientific experts – authorities on gross anatomy and marine biology – from the university. The gang of youths and most of the people on the giant climbed down, leaving behind a few hardy spirits perched on the tips of the toes and on the forehead. The experts strode around the giant, heads nodding in vigorous consultation, preceded by the policemen who pushed back the press of spectators. When they reached the outstretched hand the senior officer offered to assist them up on to the palm, but the experts hastily demurred.

After they returned to the shore, the crowd once more climbed on to the giant, and was in full possession when we left at five o'clock, covering the arms and legs like a dense flock of gulls sitting on the corpse of a large fish.

I next visited the beach three days later. My friends at the library had returned to their work, and delegated to me the task of keeping the giant under observation and preparing a report. Perhaps they sensed my particular interest in the case, and it was certainly true that I was eager to return to the beach. There was nothing necrophilic about this, for to all intents the giant was still alive for me, indeed more alive than many of the people watching him. What I found so fascinating was partly his immense scale, the huge volumes of space occupied by his arms and legs, which seemed to confirm the identity of my own miniature limbs, but above all the mere categorical fact of his existence. Whatever else in our lives might be open to doubt, the giant, dead or alive, existed in an absolute sense, providing a glimpse into a world of similar absolutes of which we spectators on the beach were such imperfect and puny copies.

When I arrived at the beach the crowd was considerably smaller, and some two or three hundred people sat on the shingle, picnicking and watching the groups of visitors who walked out across the sand. The successive tides had carried the giant nearer the shore, swinging his head and shoulders towards the beach, so that he seemed doubly to gain in size, his huge body dwarfing the fishing boats beached beside his feet. The uneven contours of the beach had pushed his spine into a slight arch, expanding his chest and tilting back the head, forcing him into a more expressly heroic posture. The combined effects of seawater and the tumefaction of the tissues had given the face a sleeker and less youthful look. Although the vast proportions of the features made it impossible to assess the age and character of the giant, on my previous visit his classically modelled mouth and nose suggested that he had been a young man of discreet and modest temper. Now, however, he appeared to be at least in early middle age. The puffy cheeks, thicker nose and temples and narrowing eyes gave him a look of well-fed maturity that even now hinted at a growing corruption to come.

This accelerated post-mortem development of the giant's character, as if the latent elements of his personality had gained sufficient momentum during his life to discharge themselves in a brief final resumé, continued to fascinate me. It marked the beginning of the giant's surrender to that all-demanding system of time in which the rest of humanity finds itself, and of which, like the million twisted ripples of a fragmented whirlpool, our finite lives are the concluding products. I took up my position on the shingle directly opposite the giant's head, from where I could see the new arrivals and the children clambering over the legs and arms.

Among the morning's visitors were a number of men in leather jackets and cloth caps, who peered up critically at the giant with a professional eye, pacing out his dimensions and making rough calculations in the sand with spars of driftwood. I assumed them to be from the public works department and other municipal bodies, no doubt wondering how to dispose of this gargantuan piece of jetsam.

Several rather more smartly attired individuals, circus proprietors and the like, also appeared on the scene, and strolled slowly around the giant, hands in the pockets of their long overcoats saying nothing to one another. Evidently its bulk was too great even for their matchless enterprise. After they had gone the children continued to run up and down the arms and legs, and the youths wrestled with each other over the supine face, the damp sand from their feet covering the white skin.

The following day I deliberately postponed my visit until the late afternoon, and when I arrived there were fewer than fifty or sixty people sitting on the shingle. The giant had been carried still closer to the shore, and was now little more than seventy-five yards away, his feet crushing the palisade of a rotting breakwater. The slope of the firmer sand tilted his body towards the sea, and the bruised face was averted in an almost conscious gesture. I sat down on a large metal winch which had been shackled to a concrete caisson above the shingle, and looked down at the recumbent figure.

His blanched skin had now lost its pearly translucence and was spattered with dirty sand which replaced that washed away by the night tide. Clumps of seaweed filled the intervals between the fingers and a collection of litter and cuttle bones lay in the crevices below the hips and knees. But despite this, and the continuous thickening of his features, the giant still retained his magnificent Homeric stature. The enormous breadth of the shoulders, and the huge columns of the arms and legs, still carried the figure into another dimension, and the giant seemed a more authentic image of one of the drowned Argonauts or heroes of the Odyssey than the conventional human-sized portrait previously in my mind.

I stepped down on to the sand, and walked between the pools of water towards the giant. Two small boys were sitting in the well of the ear, and at the far end a solitary youth stood perched high on one of the toes, surveying me as I approached. As I had hoped when delaying my visit, no one else paid any attention to me, and the people on the shore remained huddled beneath their coats.

The giant's supine right hand was covered with broken shells and sand, in which a score of footprints were visible. The rounded bulk of the hip towered above me, cutting off all sight of the sea. The sweetly acrid odour I had noticed before was now more pungent, and through the opaque skin I could see the serpentine coils of congealed blood vessels. However repellent it seemed, this ceaseless metamorphosis, visible life in death, alone permitted me to set foot on the corpse.

Using the jutting thumb as a stair-rail, I climbed up on to the palm and began my ascent. The skin was harder than I expected, barely yielding to my weight. Quickly I walked up the sloping forearm and the bulging balloon of the biceps. The face of the drowned giant loomed to my right, the cavernous nostrils and huge flanks of the cheeks like the cone of some freakish volcano.

Safely rounding the shoulder, I stepped out on to the broad promenade of the chest, across which the bony ridges of the rib-cage lay like huge rafters. The white skin was dappled by the darkening bruises of countless footprints, in which the patterns of individual heel-marks were clearly visible. Someone had built a small sandcastle on the centre of the sternum, and I climbed on to this partly demolished structure to give myself a better view of the face.

The two children had now scaled the ear and were pulling themselves into the right orbit, whose blue globe, completely occluded by some milk-coloured fluid, gazed sightlessly past their miniature forms. Seen obliquely from below, the face was devoid of all grace and repose, the drawn mouth and raised chin propped up by its gigantic slings of muscles resembling the torn prow of a colossal wreck. For the first time I became aware of the extremity of this last physical agony of the giant, no less painful for his unawareness of the collapsing musculature and tissues. The absolute isolation of the ruined figure, cast like an abandoned ship upon the empty shore, almost out of sound of the waves, transformed his face into a mask of exhaustion and helplessness.

As I stepped forward, my foot sank into a trough of soft tissue, and a gust of fetid gas blew through an aperture between the ribs. Retreating from the fouled air, which hung like a cloud over my head, I turned towards the sea to clear my lungs. To my surprise I saw that the giant's left hand had been amputated.

I stared with bewilderment at the blackening stump, while the solitary youth reclining on his aerial perch a hundred feet away surveyed me with a sanguinary eye.

This was only the first of a sequence of depredations. I spent the following two days in the library, for some reason reluctant to visit the shore, aware that I had probably witnessed the approaching end of a magnificent illusion. When I next crossed the dunes and set foot on the shingle the giant was little more than twenty yards away, and with this close proximity to the rough pebbles all traces had vanished of the magic which once surrounded his distant wave-washed form. Despite his immense size, the bruises and dirt that covered his body made him appear merely human in scale, his vast dimensions only increasing his vulnerability.

His right hand and foot had been removed, dragged up the slope and trundled away by cart. After questioning the small group of people huddled by the breakwater, I gathered that a fertilizer company and a cattle food manufacturer were responsible.

The giant's remaining foot rose into the air, a steel hawser fixed to the large toe, evidently in preparation for the following day. The surrounding beach had been disturbed by a score of workmen, and deep ruts marked the ground where the hands and foot had been hauled away. A dark brackish fluid leaked from the stumps, and stained the sand and the white cones of the cuttlefish. As I walked down the shingle I noticed that a number of jocular slogans, swastikas and other signs had been cut into the grey skin, as if the mutilation of this motionless colossus had released a sudden flood of repressed spite. The lobe of one of the ears was pierced by a spear of timber, and a small fire had burnt out in the centre of the chest, blackening the surrounding skin. The fine wood ash was still being scattered by the wind.

A foul smell enveloped the cadaver, the undisguisable signature of putrefaction, which had at last driven away the usual gathering of youths. I returned to the shingle and climbed up on to the winch. The giant's swollen cheeks had now almost closed his eyes, drawing the lips back in a monumental gape. The once straight Grecian nose had been twisted and flattened, stamped into the ballooning face by countless heels.

When I visited the beach the following day I found, almost with relief, that the head had been removed.

Some weeks elapsed before I made my next journey to the beach, and by then the human likeness I had noticed earlier had vanished again. On close inspection the recumbent thorax and abdomen were unmistakably manlike, but as each of the limbs was chopped off, first at the knee and elbow, and then at shoulder and thigh, the carcass resembled that of any headless sea-animal – whale or whale-shark. With this loss of identity, and the few traces of personality that had clung tenuously to the figure, the interest of the spectators expired, and the foreshore was deserted except for an elderly beachcomber and the watchman sitting in the doorway of the contractor's hut.

A loose wooden scaffolding had been erected around the carcass, from which a dozen ladders swung in the wind, and the surrounding sand was littered with coils of rope, long metal-handled knives and grappling irons, the pebbles oily with blood and pieces of bone and skin.

I nodded to the watchman, who regarded me dourly over his brazier of burning coke. The whole area was pervaded by the pungent smell of huge squares of blubber being simmered in a vat behind the hut.

Both the thigh-bones had been removed, with the assistance of a small crane draped in the gauze-like fabric which had once covered the waist of the giant, and the open sockets gaped like barn doors. The upper arms, collar bones and pudenda had likewise been dispatched. What remained of the skin over the thorax and abdomen had been marked out in parallel strips with a tar brush, and the first five or six sections had been pared away from the midriff, revealing the great arch of the rib-cage.

As I left, a flock of gulls wheeled down from the sky and alighted on the beach, picking at the stained sand with ferocious cries.

Several months later, when the news of his arrival had been generally forgotten, various pieces of the body of the dismembered giant began to reappear all over the city. Most of these were bones, which the fertilizer manufacturers had found too difficult to crush, and their massive size, and the huge tendons and discs of cartilage attached to their joints, immediately identified them. For some reason, these disembodied fragments seemed better to convey the essence of the giant's original magnificence than the bloated appendages that had been subsequently amputated. As I looked across the road at the premises of the largest wholesale merchants in the meat market, I recognized the two enormous thighbones on either side of the doorway. They towered over the porters' heads like the threatening megaliths of some primitive druidical religion, and I had a sudden vision of the giant climbing to his knees upon these bare bones and striding away through the streets of the city, picking up the scattered fragments of himself on his return journey to the sea.

A few days later I saw the left humerus lying in the entrance to one of the shipyards (its twin for several years lay on the mud among the piles below the harbour's principal commercial wharf). In the same week the mummified right hand was exhibited on a carnival float during the annual pageant of the guilds.

The lower jaw, typically, found its way to the museum of natural history. The remainder of the skull has disappeared, but is probably still lurking in the waste grounds or private gardens of the city – quite recently, while sailing down the river, I noticed two ribs of the giant forming a decorative arch in a waterside garden, possibly confused with the jawbones of a whale. A large square of tanned and tattooed skin, the size of an indian blanket, forms a backcloth to the dolls and masks in a novelty shop near the amusement park, and I have no doubt that elsewhere in the city, in the hotels or golf clubs, the mummified nose or ears of the giant hang from the wall above the fireplace. As for the immense pizzle, this ends its days in the freak museum of a circus which travels up and down the north-west. This monumental apparatus, stunning in its proportions and sometime potency, occupies a complete booth to itself. The irony is that it is wrongly identified as that of a whale, and indeed most people, even those who first saw him cast up on the shore after the storm, now remember the giant, if at all, as a large sea beast.

The remainder of the skeleton, stripped of all flesh, still rests on the sea-shore, the clutter of bleached ribs like the timbers of a derelict ship. The contractor's hut, the crane and the scaffolding have been removed, and the sand being driven into the bay along the coast has buried the pelvis and backbone. In the winter the high curved bones are deserted, battered by the breaking waves, but in the summer they provide an excellent perch for the sea-wearying gulls.

The Handsomest Drowned Man in the World

A tale for children

Gabriel Garcia Marquez

The first children who saw the dark and slinky bulge approaching through the sea let themselves think it was an enemy ship. Then they saw it had no flags or masts and they thought it was a whale. But when it washed up on the beach, they removed the clumps of seaweed, the jellyfish tentacles, and the remains of fish and flotsam, and only then did they see that it was a drowned man.

They had been playing with him all afternoon, burying him in the sand and digging him up again, when someone chanced to see them and spread the alarm in the village. The men who carried him to the nearest house noticed that he weighed more than any dead man they had ever known, almost as much as a horse, and they said to each other that maybe he'd been floating too long and the water had got into his bones. When they laid him on the floor they said he'd been taller than all other men because there was barely enough room for him in the house, but they thought that maybe the ability to keep on growing after death was part of the nature of certain drowned men. He had the smell of the sea about him and only his shape gave one to suppose that it was the corpse of a human being, because the skin was covered with a crust of mud and scales.

They did not even have to clean off his face to know that the dead man was a stranger. The village was made up of only twenty-odd wooden houses that had stone courtyards with no flowers and which were spread about on the end of a desertlike cape. There was so little land that mothers always went about with the fear that the wind could carry off their children and the few dead that the years had caused among them had to be thrown off the cliffs. But the sea was calm and bountiful and all the men fitted into seven boats. So when they found the drowned man they simply had to look at one another to see that they were all there.

That night they did not go to work at sea. While the men went to find out if anyone was missing in neighboring villages, the women stayed behind to care for the drowned man. They took the mud off with grass swabs, they removed the underwater stones entangled in his hair, and they scraped the crust off with tools used for scaling fish. As they were doing that they noticed that the vegetation on him came from faraway oceans and deep water and that his clothes were in tatters, as if he had sailed through labyrinths of coral. They noticed too that he bore his death with pride, for he did not have the lonely look of other drowned men who came out of the sea or that haggard, needy look of men who drowned in rivers. But only when they finished cleaning him off did they become aware of the kind of man he was and it left them breathless. Not only was he the tallest, strongest, most virile, and best built man they had ever seen, but even though they were looking at him there was no room for him in their imagination.

They could not find a bed in the village large enough to lay him on nor was there a table solid enough to use for his wake. The tallest men's holiday pants would not fit him, nor the fattest ones' Sunday shirts, nor the shoes of the one with the biggest feet. Fascinated by his huge size and his beauty, the women then decided to make him some pants from a large piece of sail and a shirt from some bridal brabant linen so that he could continue through his death with dignity. As they sewed, sitting in a circle and gazing at the corpse between stitches, it seemed to them that the wind had never been so steady nor the sea so restless as on that night and they supposed that the change had something to do with the dead man. They thought that if that magnificent man had lived in the village, his house would have had the widest doors, the highest ceiling, and the strongest floor, his bedstead would have been made from a midship frame held together by iron bolts, and his wife would have been the happiest woman. They thought that he would have had so much authority that he could have drawn fish out of the sea simply by calling their names and that he would have put so much work into his land that springs would have burst forth from among the rocks so that he would have been able to plant flowers on the cliffs. They secretly compared him to their own men, thinking that for all their lives theirs were incapable of doing what he could do in one night, and they ended up dismissing them deep in their hearts as the weakest, meanest, and most useless creatures on earth. They were wandering through that maze of fantasy when the oldest woman, who as the oldest had looked upon the drowned man with more compassion than passion, sighed:

'He has the face of someone called Esteban.'

It was true. Most of them had only to take another look at him to see that he could not have any other name. The more stubborn among them, who were the youngest, still lived for a few hours with the illusion that when they put his clothes on and he lay among the flowers in patent leather shoes his name might be Lautaro. But it was a vain illusion. There had not been enough canvas, the poorly cut and worse sewn pants were too tight, and the hidden strength of his heart popped the buttons on his shirt. After midnight the whistling of the wind died down and the sea fell into its Wednesday drowsiness. The silence put an end to any last doubts: he was Esteban. The women who had dressed him, who had combed his hair, had cut his nails and shaved him were unable to hold back a shudder of pity when they had to resign themselves to his being dragged along the ground. It was then that they understood how unhappy he must have been with that huge body since it bothered him even after death. They could see him in life, condemned to going through doors sideways, cracking his head on crossbeams, remaining on his feet during visits, not knowing what to do with his soft, pink, sea lion hands while the lady of the house looked for her most resistant chair and begged him, frightened to death, sit here, Esteban, please, and he, leaning against the wall, smiling, don't bother, ma'am, I'm fine where I am, his heels raw and his back roasted from having done the same thing so many times whenever he paid a visit, don't bother, ma'am, I'm fine where I am, just to avoid the embarrassment of breaking up the chair, and never knowing perhaps that the ones who said don't go, Esteban, at least wait till the coffee's ready, were the ones who later on would whisper the big boob finally left, how nice, the handsome fool has gone. That was what the women were thinking beside the body a little before dawn. Later, when they covered his face with a handkerchief so that the light would not bother him, he looked so forever dead, so defenseless, so much like their men that the first furrows of tears opened in their hearts. It was one of the younger ones who began the weeping. The others coming to, went from sighs to wails, and the more they sobbed the more they felt like weeping, because the drowned man was becoming all the more Esteban for them, and so they wept so much, for he was the most destitute, most peaceful, and most obliging man on earth, poor Esteban. So when the men returned with the news that the drowned man was not from the neighboring villages either, the women felt an opening of jubilation in the midst of their tears.

'Praise the Lord,' they sighed, 'he's ours!'

The men thought the fuss was only womanish frivolity. Fatigued because of the difficult night-time inquiries, all they wanted was to get rid of the bother of the newcomer once and for all before the sun grew strong on that arid, windless day. They improvised a litter with the remains of foremasts and gaffs, tying it together with rigging so that it would bear the weight of the body until they reached the cliffs. They wanted to tie the anchor from a cargo ship to him so that he would sink easily into the deepest waves, where fish are blind and divers die of nostalgia, and bad currents would not bring him back to shore, as had happened with other bodies. But the more they hurried, the more the women thought of ways to waste time. They walked about like startled hens, pecking with the sea charms on their breasts, some interfering on one side to put a scapular of the good wind on the drowned man, some on the other side to put a wrist compass on him, and after a great deal of *get away from there, woman, stay out of the way, look, you almost made me fall on top of the dead man*, the men began to feel mistrust in their livers and started grumbling about why so many main-altar decorations for a stranger, because no matter how many nails and holy-water jars he had on him, the sharks would chew him all the same, but the women kept piling on their junk relics, running back and forth, stumbling, while they released in sighs what they did not in tears, so that the men finally exploded with *since when has there ever been such a fuss over a drifting corpse, a drowned nobody, a piece of cold Wednesday meat*. One of the women, mortified by so much lack of care, then removed the handkerchief from the dead man's face and the men were left breathless too.

He was Esteban. It was not necessary to repeat it for them to recognize him. If they had been told Sir Walter Raleigh even they might have been impressed with his gringo accent, the macaw on his shoulder, his cannibal-killing blunderbuss, but there could be only one Esteban in the world and there he was, stretched out like a sperm whale, shoeless, wearing the pants of an undersized child, and with those stony nails that had to be cut with a knife. They only had to take the handkerchief off his face to see that he was ashamed, that it was not his fault that he was so big or so heavy or so handsome, and if he had known that this was going to happen, he would have looked for a more discreet place to drown in, seriously, I even would have tied the anchor off a galleon around my neck and staggered off a cliff like someone who doesn't like things in order not to be upsetting people now with this Wednesday dead body, as you people say, in order not to be bothering anyone with this filthy piece of cold meat that doesn't have anything to do with me. There was so much truth in his manner that even the most mistrustful men, the ones who felt the bitterness of endless nights at sea fearing that their women would tire of dreaming about them and begin to dream of drowned men, even they and others who were harder still shuddered in the marrow of their bones at Esteban's sincerity.

That was how they came to hold the most splendid funeral they could conceive of for an abandoned drowned man. Some women who had gone to get flowers in the neighboring villages returned with other women who could not believe what they had been told, and those women went back for more flowers when they saw the dead man, and they brought more and more until there were so many flowers and so many people that it was hard to walk about. At the final moment it pained them to return him to the waters as an orphan and they chose a father and mother from among the best people, and aunts and uncles and cousins, so that through him all the inhabitants of the village became kinsmen. Some sailors who heard the weeping from a distance went off course and people heard of one who had himself tied to the mainmast, remembering ancient fables about sirens. While they fought for the privilege of carrying him on their shoulders along the steep escarpment by the cliffs, men and women became aware for the first time of the desolation of their streets, the dryness of their courtyards, the narrowness of their dreams as they faced the splendor and beauty of their drowned man. They let him go without an anchor so that he could come back if he wished and whenever he wished, and they all held their breath for the fraction of centuries the body took to fall into the abyss. They did not need to look at one another to realize that they were no longer all present, that they would never be. But they also knew that everything would be different from then on, that their houses would have wider doors, higher ceilings, and stronger floors so that Esteban's memory could go everywhere without bumping into beams and so that no one in the future would dare whisper the big boob finally died, too bad, the handsome fool has finally died, because they were going to paint their house fronts gay colors to make Esteban's memory eternal and they were going to break their backs digging for springs among the stones and planting flowers on the cliffs so that in future years at dawn the passengers on great liners would awaken, suffocated by the smell of gardens on the high seas, and the captain would have to come down from the bridge in his dress uniform, with his astrolabe, his pole star, and his row of war medals and, pointing to the promontory of roses on the horizon, he would say in fourteen languages, look there, where the wind is so peaceful now that it's gone to sleep beneath the beds, over there, where the sun's so bright that the sunflowers don't know which way to turn, yes, over there, that's Esteban's village.

Commentary

Games at Twilight   *Anita Desai*

Anita Desai was born in 1937, of a Bengali father and a German mother. She lives in the Indian city of Bombay, which is the setting for most of the stories in the collection *Games at Twilight* (1978), from which this story is taken. Like many other contemporary Indian writers, Anita Desai writes in English. Other books include the novels *Fire on the Mountain*, about a woman's relationship with her highly independent great-granddaughter, and *The Village by the Sea*, which concerns the experience of two older children living through the poverty of contemporary India. Children figure prominently in Desai's stories.

Ideas for discussion

Games at Twilight is set in a prosperous suburban garden in an Indian city, though the experience it describes could happen anywhere.

As a 'grown-up' reader, I find that Anita Desai's writing evokes vividly the peculiar intensity of childhood, when senses and emotions are so often 'out of control'. How is the reader made conscious of the atmosphere of this Indian garden in the late afternoon? What makes the garden shed such an alarming place for a child to hide?

Ravi's relationship with the older children is not unlike that described in the next story, *The Giant Woman*. What impressions do we get of the characters of the other children – Raghu in particular? How does Ravi fit into their world?

At its simplest, the story concerns Ravi's attempt to win a childish glory by outwitting the *older, bigger, luckier children* in a game of hide-and-seek. In the end, he is cross with himself for not winning when he perhaps could have done. The final paragraph, however, shows that something more has happened. Ravi is left crying from *a terrible sense of his insignificance*. The 'mortuary' smell of the shed is still in his nostrils, and he has been frightened by something altogether more disturbing than creepy-crawlies.

Do you understand what he feels at this point? (Does he?)

Ideas for writing

☐ *He had wanted victory and triumph – not a funeral* (p. 8). Can you explain why Ravi is so upset by what happens in *Games at Twilight*?

☐ Imagine yourself hiding in darkness, in a place that is unfamiliar to you. Write about what you experience there, and what you feel on returning to the world that you know.

☐ Write the thoughts of a ghost who returns to observe (unseen) the people she or he once lived among.

Further reading

Anita Desai: *Fire on the Mountain* (Heinemann, 1977; Penguin, 1981); *Games at Twilight* (Heinemann, 1978; Penguin, 1982); *The Village by the Sea* (Heinemann New Windmill, 1985).

Commentary

The Giant Woman *Joyce Carol Oates*

Joyce Carol Oates was born in 1938, near Lockport, in the rural back-reaches of upper New York State. She spent much of her childhood on a small farmstead owned by her grandparents. 'Eden County', which is the setting for a number of her novels and stories (*The Giant Woman* included) is the fictional equivalent of that early experience. Joyce Carol Oates is an immensely productive writer, and is already the author of a dozen books of short stories – a form in which she excels – as well as novels and poetry.

The Giant Woman is taken from *Nightside* (1976), a short story collection which explores fearful and dream-like experiences.

Ideas for discussion

As a piece of storytelling, *The Giant Woman* is unconventional, since events do not unfold in an orderly way. As so often with memories, we are not entirely sure what happened when. The first two pages are perhaps deliberately confusing, plunging the reader into the experience of being chased, apparently after trespassing. The child at the centre of the experience says little, but her feelings are vividly presented. What is her perception of 'the giant woman'? How do the older children treat the narrator?

On p. 10, the story in effect begins again, in a more traditional way. (In a film, this would be the moment when the titles appear.) At this point, it becomes clear that the narrator is not exactly the child, but rather the adult looking back. In this part of the story (p. 10–15), the readers learns more about the old woman, and the background to the previous escapade.

Mrs Mueller is clearly the kind of character about whom stories get told. She is *not like other people* (p. 12), a foreign immigrant, a recluse. (In the 17th century, she would certainly have been identified as 'a witch'.) What does the child find 'odd' about her appearance and behaviour?

The conversation on p. 14–15 acts as a kind of communal narrative – fragments, as it were, of possible stories. (The similarities between gossiping and story-writing have often been noted.) The old gossips of the neighbourhood evidently talk a good deal about Mrs Mueller. How much of it is true, do you think? Why do people feel the need to gossip in this way?

The adventure at the heart of the story starts on p. 18, but the earlier pages have prepared for it in all sorts of ways. (What does the description of the marsh and the orchard, for example, add to the story at that point?) The description of the interior of Mrs Mueller's house is carefully detailed. How does the writer convey the particular atmosphere of the house, and the children's feelings about being in it? Entering someone else's bedroom is a widely held 'taboo'. How does this come out in the story?

A turning point in the young girl's feelings seems to occur when she looks out of Mrs Mueller's window, on p. 21. Can you see why this moment is important to her? After that, she is reluctant to look any further. Why doesn't she tell Donna and Albert about the money?

At the end of the story, the girl doesn't know why she feels 'so happy'. Try and explain her feelings as she runs away from the house.

Ideas for writing

☐ Describe carefully the young girl's visit to Mrs Mueller's house, and explain the development of her feelings during the course of the visit.

☐ *Sometimes he lied and sometimes he told the truth* . . . (p. 16). Write about the time Bobbie Orkin visited Mrs Mueller's barn.

☐ 'What excites me about writing is the uses I can make of myself, of various small adventures, errors, miscalculations, stunning discoveries, near-disasters, and occasional reversals of everything, but so worked into a fictional structure that no one could guess how autobiographical it all is.' The process Joyce Carol Oates describes here is also what the brain does when it sleeps. Write something which uses vivid fragments of your experience, but re-combines them in intriguing, perhaps dream-like, ways.

Further reading

Joyce Carol Oates: *The Wheel of Love* (Gollancz, 1971); *Wild Saturday and Other Stories* (Dent Everyman, 1984); *Nightside* (Gollancz, 1979).

Next term, we'll mash you   *Penelope Lively*

Penelope Lively was born and brought up in Egypt, but settled in England after the war. She made her reputation as a writer with a series of novels for older children, of which *The Ghost of Thomas Kempe* (1973) is probably the best known. Since 1977 she has concentrated on writing adult fiction, in which the behaviour of the middle-classes is observed with shrewd understanding.

Next term, we'll mash you is from Penelope Lively's first collection of short stories, *Nothing Missing But the Samovar* (1978).

Ideas for discussion

Next term, we'll mash you leaves us in no doubt what the author thinks of Mr and Mrs Manders, and their quest for a suitable 'prep' school for their son Charles. (A prep school is a fee-paying junior boarding-school which 'prepares' children for the Public School entrance examination.) The treatment of the parents is satirical: the writer makes fun of these characters in order to demonstrate her disapproval of them.

What factors do the Manders consider in deciding where to educate Charles? What do you think Mrs Manders means by 'the schoolmaster-type' (p. 25), and what 'type' does she prefer? Why are the Wilcoxes so often mentioned?

During the course of the story, the boy Charles says nothing at all – even his internal thoughts go unrecorded. And yet the reader is in no doubt about how Charles feels at each stage of the visit. Why do you think Penelope Lively chose to make the boy 'mute' in this way? How *do* we learn what he feels about the prospect of attending such a school?

In this context, you might look closely at one aspect of the way the story is told: there's a change of style at the point where the Headmaster's wife bears Charles away (p. 28), which is maintained until he is returned to his parents – and reoccurs in the final paragraph. What is the effect of this change of style?

Commentary

Ideas for writing

☐ *After all, you're choosing a school for him, aren't you, and not for you . . .* (p. 27). How does Charles's view of the Preparatory School differ from that of his parents?

☐ When Charles has been at the school for three weeks, his parents pay him a visit. Write about this occasion.

☐ Write a story which alternates between two different styles, in order to bring out the differences between two people's experience of the same situation.

Further reading

Penelope Lively: *Going Back* (Heinemann, 1975); *Nothing Missing But the Samovar* (Heinemann, 1978).

The Exercise   *Bernard Mac Laverty*

Bernard Mac Laverty was born in Belfast in 1942. After ten years working as a laboratory technician he went to university in Belfast, then moved to Scotland to teach. He now lives on the Isle of Islay, off Western Scotland. To date he has published two outstanding collections of short stories, and two poignant and powerful novels, *Lamb* (1980) and *Cal* (1983) – the latter about a love affair caught up in the sectarian violence of contemporary Ulster.

The Exercise is from Bernard Mac Laverty's first book, *Secrets* (1977).

Ideas for discussion

The Exercise is set in Belfast in the 1950s, where Kevin Sweeney attends a Catholic boys' grammar school. (Hence the 'soutane', or priest's cassock, and the prayers that begin and end each lesson.)

One of Mac Laverty's characteristic skills as a story-teller, is his knack of bringing physical details into exceptionally sharp focus, so that the reader gains a vivid sense of the moment described, and of the feelings that attended it. For instance, how is Kevin's perception of his father built up over the first two pages?

In a sense, Kevin has two 'fathers'. One he addresses as *Father* (because Waldo is a priest), the other as *Da*. In both characters, the roles of father and teacher become superimposed, but Kevin's feelings concerning the two men are sharply distinguished. (Both the violence and the tenderness of 'father – son' relationships are explored further in *Lamb*.)

Does Kevin resent Waldo's behaviour? Does Waldo's apology cut any ice, with Kevin or with the reader? How important is the notion of social class?

On first reading, I found the last half-page of this story curiously moving, without quite knowing why. On reflection, it's to do with certain carefully chosen details, like the playful tap with the newspaper, or Kevin putting his hand in his father's pocket. Can you explain your own response to the ending? Why does Kevin not tell his father what happened about the homework?

You might compare Kevin's experience in this story with that of Roger in *Bicycles, muscles, cigarets*. What have the stories got in common?

Ideas for writing

☐ What do we learn about the relationship between Kevin and his father?

☐ Write a story based on an incident that actually occurred during one of your lessons, but substituting a fictitious teacher. You could use Waldo, or Mrs Spokes (*Next term we'll mash you*), or the teacher from Tite Comprehensive (*Broken Homes*), or a character of your own invention.

Further reading

Bernard Mac Laverty: *Secrets and Other Stories* (Blackstaff/Alison & Busby, 1977); *Lamb* (Cape, 1980; Penguin, 1981); *A Time to Dance and other stories* (Cape, 1982; Penguin, 1985); *Cal* (Cape, 1983; Penguin, 1984).

Bicycles, muscles, cigarets   *Raymond Carver*

Raymond Carver was born in Clatskanie, Oregon, USA, in 1939. He has published several books of poetry, but he is chiefly known as a writer of unusually condensed and powerful short stories. The world of Raymond Carver's fiction is the underside of 'The American Dream'. For the most part, his characters lead sad, inarticulate lives, complicated by twists of emotion they only half-understand; success stories are few, and happiness hard-won.

Bicycles, muscles, cigarets was published in *Will You Please Be Quiet, Please* (1976).

Ideas for discussion

Far more than with other stories, the style in which *Bicycles, muscles, cigarets* is written is fundamental to the effect it creates. At first, the writing may appear merely flat, even artless. Carver uses a limited vocabulary, and only the simplest sentences. Typically, the action is built up through a series of low-key conversations, recorded with remarkable fidelity to what people actually say. It is a style in which 'the narrator' has entirely disappeared: that is, we are not aware of an author-figure judging or commenting upon the behaviour described. The spareness which the writer achieves, and the consequent sense of all that has been suppressed, is the source of the story's power.

How is the 'ordinariness' of the experience established in the first half of the story? At this stage, where is the reader's interest focused?

Mrs Miller says: *How do you know who or what to believe?* Which of the boys, if any, did you think might be telling the truth?

Reread the story carefully from Mr Berman's arrival to the struggle on the lawn. In what ways is Berman's behaviour *out of line* with that of the other two adults present? How much provocation is Hamilton offered?

How did you react to Hamilton's attack on Berman? Was it expected, justifiable, believable? Why did he do it? How did he feel about it afterwards?

Unusually in this anthology, the child's experience is seen from the parent's point of view. Can we guess what's going through Roger's mind over the last few pages? Why does he suddenly want to talk about his grandfather?

Does the rather odd title of this story alert you to anything about it?

Commentary

Ideas for writing

☐ Discuss Evan Hamilton's experience in *Bicycles, muscles, cigarets*.

☐ Write two conversations that occur the following day. The first is a public conversation involving Roger, Kip and Gary Berman. The second is a private conversation involving Roger and Kip.

☐ Write about an incident in which the pattern of ordinary social behaviour is disrupted by behaviour of a wholly unexpected kind.

Further reading

Raymond Carver: *The Stories of Raymond Carver* (Picador, 1985).

Red Dress – 1946   *Alice Munro*

Alice Munro grew up in the semi-rural landscape of Southern Ontario, Canada, where she still lives, and where almost all her stories are set. She has written consistently about the settled, 'ordinary' lives of small-town communities, and especially about growing up in such a world. Alice Munro's stories often seem like fragments of her own remembered past, or the communal biography of the people among whom she has lived. Besides her four volumes of short stories, she has also written a novel in the form of a sequence of stories, *Lives of Girls and Women* (1971).

Red Dress – 1946 is from Alice Munro's first collection of stories, *Dance of the Happy Shades* (1968).

Ideas for discussion

The narrator of *Red Dress – 1946* is an unnamed thirteen-year-old whom we may reasonably call 'Alice'. The extent to which these things 'actually happened' to the real Alice Munro is something we can never know, though the date in the title, as well as the quality of the writing, suggest at least an element of autobiography.

The girl's relationship with her mother is clearly at a point of change. What is it that now 'embarrasses' her about her mother? What are her feelings about the dress? Why is she angry when her mother says *Au reservoir*?

Alice says she longed to be *back safe behind the boundaries of childhood* (p. 50). What seem to be the reasons for this insecurity? How does it show itself? What does Lonnie's friendship mean to her?

Do you think Alice's mother is trying to encourage her emergence from childhood, or wanting to delay it? What is the importance of the 'red dress' (and the lace collar) in this context?

The story concentrates on Alice's perception of herself. (*There was something mysterious the matter with me . . .*) Do you think others see her as she imagines they do – at the dance, for example?

Alice's view of Mary Fortune is quite complex. She notes, for instance, that the older girl *has suffered the same defeats as I had* (p. 55). What does it mean to her to smoke and talk to Mary in the janitor's room, while the dance continues?

At the point where she is about to leave the dance, Alice says confidently: *I was not waiting for anybody to choose me. I had my own plans.* (p. 55). Were you pleased for her at this point? At the end, she says: *I went round the house to the back door, thinking, I have been to a dance and a boy has walked me home and kissed me. It was all true. My life was possible* (p. 56). Do you regard the outcome of the evening as a kind of victory, or a kind of defeat? How does Raymond Bolting rate as a boyfriend? Does it matter?

The last paragraph (as so often in a short story) draws together a number of strands in the girl's experience. The final sentence needs particular thought. Do you understand what Alice Munro means?

Ideas for writing

□ *I was close to despair at all times* ... (p. 48). What has the onset of adolescence meant to the girl in *Red Dress – 1946*, and what is the significance, for her, of the events she describes?

□ Write a series of short, first-person accounts which give other people's views of events that evening: Mason Williams's account of the first dance; Mary Fortune's account of the meeting in the washroom; Raymond Bolting's account of walking a girl home.

□ Write a story based on an occasion when you have yourself felt particularly self-conscious. 'Fictionalise' the experience if you wish (perhaps writing about yourself in the third person) but include as many details taken from what actually happened, as you can remember.

Further reading

Alice Munro: *Dance of the Happy Shades* (Ryerson, 1968; Penguin, 1983); *Lives of Girls and Women* (Penguin, 1982); *The Beggar Maid* (Penguin, 1980).

Gold Dust   *George Mackay Brown*

George Mackay Brown was born in Stromness, Orkney, in 1921, and has lived there virtually all his life. He is probably best known as a poet, but he has also written novels, plays, and several volumes of short stories, many of which relate to the history, both past and present, of the Orkney people. His work in all these modes is marked by a rich sense of ceremony and tradition, and an alert ear for the language of living communities.

Gold Dust is one of a group of stories published in the volume *Andrina* (1983).

Ideas for discussion

The connection between fiction and gossip is well established (see also the commentary on *The Giant Woman*), and the first half of *Gold Dust* is composed almost entirely of the things the characters say about each other. What is the local opinion (Mrs Scully, Mr Somerville, Ida Innes) of Frank Kern?

What sort of woman is Bridie, Frank's mother? Are the gossips right about her? Why does the publication of the poem mean so much to her?

The style in which the story is written is one which George Mackay Brown

Commentary

has made very much his own. There is a hard-won simplicity here, an uncluttered attentiveness to things and events, which is characteristic of the writer's best poetry. The narrative or story-telling technique is also interesting: a sequence of 'snap-shot' images linked to revealing fragments of overheard conversation, with a strong sense of 'cutting' from scene to scene. The influence of the cinema on modern story-telling is strongly apparent.

Do you notice a slight 'change of key' with the entry of the postman on p. 60, followed by the appearance of Frank himself? What effect do you think the writer is aiming for at this point in the story?

In the bar of 'The Lion of Scotland', 'The Poet' carries off his new role in some style. How does the writer want us to react to Frank Kern? Do we share Frank's pleasure in his own success? Is he a ridiculous figure? How does the tone of the story effect our judgement? Is our response to Frank influenced by our feeling about the rest of the community?

Ideas for writing

□ What opinion of Frank Kern did you derive from your reading of *Gold Dust*, and what led you to that conclusion?

□ Mr Paton finishes his vodka and orange. He steps out into Chapel Street, where he exchanges brief words with Bridie Kern, and then (crossing the street) with Mrs Scully. Shortly afterwards, Mrs Scully finds occasion to visit Mr Somerville's grocery store. Write these conversations, borrowing the style of the original story.

□ Write some of Frank Kern's poems.

Further reading

George Mackay Brown: *A Calendar of Love* (Hogarth Press, 1967; Triad, 1978); *A Time to Keep* (Hogarth Press, 1969); *Greenvoe* (Penguin, 1976); *Selected Poems* (Hogarth Press, 1977); *Andrina* (Granada, 1984).

Broken Homes   *William Trevor*

William Trevor was born in County Cork, in southern Ireland, in 1928. In the last twenty years he has published five collections of short stories, and a good number of novels. As a writer, his special province has been the lives of 'ordinary' people, often living in small backwaters – first in Ireland, and later in England, where he now lives. As a wry chronicler of the surface details of social life – what people wear, how people talk – Trevor has few equals; what also absorbs him is the vein of 'quiet desperation' which he finds running just below that surface.
Broken Homes is from the collection *Lovers of Their Time* (1978).

Ideas for discussion

Broken Homes is a story about 'the generation gap' – or, less simply, about the 'gaps' that can open up between people of any age, when *conversation breaks down between them*. Why do the teacher and Mrs Malby have such difficulty understanding each other? What is it about the teacher's appearance and behaviour that makes Mrs Malby uncomfortable? (Which of the two communicates more clearly?)

The behaviour and conversation of the four 'kids' is precisely observed, and always through Mrs Malby's eyes. Did this give you a different view of youth and its culture? Can we tell what William Trevor thinks of them?

How much of a comfort to Mrs Malby are the Kings? Is there a gap of any kind between the old lady and her helpful neighbours? Do they gain the reader's sympathy?

At several points in the story, Mrs Malby's mind goes back to 1942, to the death of her sons. Do you understand why she should be reminded of the past in this way? What are the things that mean most to Mrs Malby? What most upsets her? Can you explain why she puts up so little resistance?

Mrs Malby is conscious on occasions how 'dream-like' (or nightmarish) the experience is becoming. Do you believe all this could happen 'in real life'?

William Trevor's style is highly distinctive. He achieves, it seems to me, a particular kind of flatness in the author's voice, which implies that a great deal has been left unsaid. This comes over, for example, in his habit of listing things (as in the list of visitors on p. 65), or in the way much of the conversation goes into reported speech, which somehow removes everything from language except its content (*The voice reminded its listeners that it was the voice of Pete Murray* p. 68.) What aspects of the style of the writing did you notice in your reading of the story?

The policy is to foster a deeper understanding. Between the generations, says the teacher at the beginning of the story. By the end of it, the reader knows the kind of things about Mrs Malby which might have helped the pupils – or the teacher – to reach that 'deeper understanding'. About the *kids from broken homes*, however, the reader learns scarcely anything. If we knew what the kids thought was going on, might that put the matter in a different light – or not?

Ideas for writing

□ *The policy is to foster a deeper understanding.* Why is the policy so unsuccessful?

□ Pupils who go on community placements are often required to write up a log-book describing what they did. Write a detailed log-book entry for that Tuesday, done by one of the four kids involved.

□ A: *Got that, Billo? Washing walls.* B: *Who loves ya, baby?*
Write a life-like conversation in which people talk a good deal, but actually communicate very little.

Further reading

William Trevor: *Elizabeth Alone* (Bodley Head, 1973; Panther, 1977); *Children of Dynmouth* (Bodley Head, 1976; Penguin, 1979; Heinemann New Windmill, 1981); *The Stories of William Trevor* (Penguin, 1983).

KBW   *Farrukh Dhondy*

Farrukh Dhondy was born in Poona, in India, and came to Britain as an undergraduate in the 1960s. He then taught for some years in London schools. In the 1970s he wrote two books of short stories for teenagers – *East End at Your Feet* and *Come to Mecca* – which dealt frankly with the experiences of young British Asians living in inner London, both from their own viewpoint, and from that of their white neighbours. He is now a television editor for Channel 4.

KBW is from Farrukh Dhondy's first book, *East End at Your Feet* (1976).

Ideas for discussion

From what he says (and from the way he says it), the twelve-year-old narrator of *KBW* gives us a clear idea of the kind of lad he is. What do he and Tahir have in common? What impression do you get of life on the Devonmount estate? How does the narrator feel about living there?

The boy's dad is clearly well-known in the locality for his political views. He refers on p. 86 to the fact that in the 1930s, during the period of mass unemployment, there was a campaign of violence in the East End directed against Jewish 'immigrants', and led by the British Fascist party (some of whose members later founded the National Front). Why does the Dad talk of 'anti-working class prejudices'? Do you understand the connection between being a Communist and befriending the Habibs?

The mother's attitude to politics, and to the Habibs, is rather different. How would you describe it? (Does she share the same opinions as Mrs Biggles, for example?)

What do you think is going through Tahir's mind during the incident with the cocoa? Why does the boy Alan look 'like a dog that's been whipped'? Is the narrator guilty of betraying Tahir? Do you sympathise with Tahir's decision to leave the cricket club? (Why *do* local people connect the outbreak of typhoid with the Habibs?)

What kind of bloody Communist are you? demands the mother (p. 87) *I knew what he felt*, says the son. Would you call the father a coward? Did he betray his principles? Why wouldn't he attend Jenny's funeral?

Ideas for writing

□ *I still think I was his best friend* (p.82). Describe the friendship between the narrator and Tahir in *KBW*, and explain how it comes to be destroyed.

□ Explain the differences in political attitude between the mother and the father in *KBW*.

□ Tahir and the narrator did not speak to each other about what had happened, though each thought he could guess the other's feelings. Imagine they meet up again a few years later, and write their conversation.

Further reading

Farrukh Dhondy: *East End at your Feet* (MacMillan Topliner, 1976); *Come to Mecca* (Collins, 1978; Fontana Lion, 1978); *The Siege of Babylon* (MacMillan Topliner Red Star, 1978).

Nineteen Fifty-Five   *Alice Walker*

Alice Walker was born in Georgia, in the 'deep south' of America, in 1944. She is a black feminist writer, whose poetry, novels and stories engage with the double oppression of being black and being a woman in a society in which both conditions can be made to count heavily against you. Her heroes are the black female singers of the early twentieth century, who sang out of that same experience, and in so doing won themselves the possibility of a new status, and a new freedom. Because Alice Walker's fiction is written out of the lives of the people she has known and talked with, her voice is in a real sense the voice of a people, and of a movement.

Nineteen Fifty-Five is taken from Alice Walker's second collection of stories, *You Can't Keep a Good Woman Down* (1981).

Ideas for discussion

Nineteen Fifty-Five is a story which mixes history and fiction in a way typical of this writer's work. Johnny Carson, for example, is a real person, as was Bessie Smith, one of the greatest of American Blues artists. Gracie May and Traynor are both invented – except that Traynor's career bears a more than coincidental resemblance to the career of Elvis Presley, the most famous of the white exponents of black music, who died in 1977.

The story is a striking example of a first-person narrative, in which the vigorously idiomatic language that Gracie Mae uses, suggests a whole way of looking at the world. When stories take the form of direct personal speech (or personal writing) the reader is simultaneously aware of what is being reported, and of the character and attitude of the person reporting it.

What sense do we get of Gracie May's way of life? How troubled is she by her fatness, for example? What is her attitude to wealth and success, or her relationship with the men she lives with? Is she a good-humoured woman?

Can you explain why Traynor is so dissatisfied with the life which success has brought him? Why do his beautiful house and his beautiful wife mean so little to him? What does he think of his fans?

The relationship between Gracie Mae and Traynor is an unusual one. What does she mean to him? Why does he shower her with impossible presents, and why is he so keen that she should sing the song on the Johnny Carson Show? What does Traynor mean to Gracie Mae?

About the song itself we learn nothing directly, though Traynor often asks Gracie Mae about it. Do you have any sense of what kind of song it must have been?

In the dedication to *You Can't Keep a Good Woman Down*, Alice Walker thanks Bessie Smith and other black singers of that generation for having shown her *the value and beauty of the authentic*, and it seems helpful to consider the story in those terms. How *authentic* is Traynor? What does Gracie Mae have in mind when she says, at the end, *One day this is going to be a pitiful country*?

Commentary

Ideas for writing

☐ Why is Gracie Mae's life happier than Traynor's?

☐ Put yourself in the place of one of Traynor's fans in the audience at the Johnny Carson Show when Traynor and Gracie Mae appear (p.101–2). Write a letter to a friend describing what happened on the show, and how you felt about it.

☐ Write a song for Traynor to sing, which puts into words the nature of the life he leads, and the things that trouble him about it.

Further reading

Alice Walker: *Meridian* (Women's Press, 1982); *You Can't Keep a Good Woman Down* (Women's Press, 1982); *The Color Purple* (Women's Press, 1983).

Country Lovers   *Nadine Gordimer*

Nadine Gordimer was born in 1923 in a small town near Johannesburg, South Africa, where her parents were European immigrants. She is a writer of fiction who has won international praise for her compelling accounts of lives lived under the South African system of 'apartheid' (or 'separate development'), which confines wealth and power to a privileged white minority. Her novels and stories deal powerfully and sympathetically with the struggle for dignity and freedom waged by both black and white opponents of the South African regime.

Country Lovers is from the collection *A Soldier's Embrace* (1980), where it was published together with a companion piece, *City Lovers*, under the joint title *Town and Country Lovers*. Both stories also appear in the excellent short selection of Nadine Gordimer's South African stories, *Six Feet of the Country*.

Ideas for discussion

Until 1985, sexual relations between members of different races were forbidden in South Africa: even kissing was punishable by imprisonment. This is not directly stated in the story, but from the start the secretive nature of Paulus and Thebedi's courtship makes the situation clear.

We learn that black and white friendships established on the farm during childhood do not persist into adolescence. What brings about this change? And what is it in the case of Paulus and Thebedi that allows such feelings to survive childhood? Does the reader approve of their secret affair?

There are at least three ways in which Paulus is the dominant partner in the relationship: he is white, he is male, and he is the son of Thebedi's master. The extent to which Thebedi 'looks up' to him is made clear. Does Paulus take advantage of Thebedi's relative vulnerability? Are the two young people equally to blame for what happens? Is Thebedi – as the court suspects – an *accomplice*?

When Paulus comes out of the hut after poisoning the child, he walks away *with plodding stride (his father's gait) out of sight, towards his father's house* (p. 110). Is there significance in the emphasis on the father at this point?

Events during the court hearings are perhaps surprising. Why might Thebedi have said what she did on the occasion of the first hearing? And why should she then contradict herself a year later – thereby committing *perjury* (i.e. lying in court) on one occasion or the other? What impression does the story give of the South African legal system?

It is worth pausing over the style in which this story is written. There is very little direct conversation, for example – apart from the intense exchange on p. 109. Nor do we see inside the thoughts of either character. Their behaviour is reported from the outside, by someone who knows in detail what happened, but remains factual and detached. Why might Nadine Gordimer have chosen to tell the story in this way?

In the newspaper, Thebedi is quoted as saying, *It was a thing of our childhood* . . Was it? What feelings does the story leave you with? Do you find it easy to pass judgement on what happened?

Ideas for writing

□ Write about the ways in which natural feelings come into conflict with the South African social system in *Country Lovers*.

□ Years later, Paulus talks to a friend, for the first time, about the experiences described in *Country Lovers*. Write the conversation.

□ Select a 'human interest' item from a newspaper. Use your imagination to reconstruct the story which resulted in the newspaper report (it would be best not to use the original names). In the last paragraph of your story, quote directly from the report.

Further reading

Nadine Gordimer: *The Conservationist* (Cape, 1974; Penguin, 1978); *No Place Like: Selected Short Stories* (Cape, 1975; Penguin, 1978); *July's People* (Cape, 1981; Penguin, 1982); *Six Feet of the Country* (Penguin, 1982).

Civil Peace   *Chinua Achebe*

Chinua Achebe was born in 1930, in Eastern Nigeria. His mother-tongue is Ibo, but he began to learn English in his childhood (Nigeria was at one time a British territory), and writes in the English language. Achebe's first and best-known novel, *Things Fall Apart* (1958), concerns the impact upon traditional Ibo culture of the 'civilising' efforts of British missionaries in the days of the Empire, and his work as a whole offers a sustained account of Nigeria's history. In 1967, Achebe's Eastern (Ibo) Province attempted to break away from federal Nigeria, calling itself the Republic of Biafra. There followed three years of massacre, famine and civil war. Biafra rejoined Nigeria in 1970.

The collection *Girls at War* (1972), from which the story *Civil Peace* is taken, contains a number of stories relating to the Biafran War.

A Note on Pidgin English. Readers unacquainted with African (or West Indian) dialect-forms may at first find the passages of conversation in this story difficult to follow. Pidgin English is not 'bad' English, but a particular local form of it. It is an oral (spoken) dialect, and the meaning should become clear when the lines are read aloud. For example: 'ex gratia' payment (i.e. 'thank-you' money), becomes *egg-rasher*. *Na* means 'it is'; *wetin* means 'what thing'; *say* means 'that', or 'if'; and *am-o* means 'it'.

Ideas for discussion

In *Civil Peace* Chinua Achebe makes us aware in all kinds of ways of the state of the country following the war. It is a world, for example, in which only soldiers have 'good' money. What details best convey to you the conditions in post-war Biafra, and the lives of its inhabitants?

Not everyone in Jonathan Iwegbu's position would consider themselves *extraordinarily lucky*, but what others might see as small mercies, Jonathan sees as *miracles*. His motto is: *Nothing puzzles God.* What does he mean by this? Is there a saying in your own culture that means more or less the same?

Despite the immensity of the Biafran tragedy, there are comic elements in this tale. Do you find the tone of the story achieves any particular effect? What are the implications of the phrase *civil peace*, as the robber uses it? How is the reader led to feel about the loss of the £20?

Ideas for writing

☐ What picture emerges from this story of the state of Biafra in the aftermath of the civil war, and what is Jonathan Iwegbu's attitude towards this state of affairs?

☐ Most robberies are committed upon the poor, by the very poor. Write about an encounter between robber and victim, from the robber's point of view.

Further reading

Chinua Achebe: *Things Fall Apart* (Heinemann, 1958); *Girls at War* (Heinemann, 1972).

The Drowned Giant   *J G Ballard*

J G Ballard was born in Shanghai in 1930. After the war his family returned to England, where he trained in medicine. In the late 1950s he began to publish the science fiction stories which have earned him a reputation as one of the most original post-war English writers. In Ballard's hands, there is much more to 'sci-fi' than bug-eyed monsters or intergalactic shoot-outs. His work is political in the widest sense: Ballard's novels and stories, which are almost always disturbing, may be set far into an unidentified future, but they invite us to reflect deeply on the world we already have. He has also written *Empire of the Sun*, a novel based on his experience of a Japanese prison camp.

The Drowned Giant is taken from *The Terminal Beach* (1964).

Ideas for discussion

The phrase *the willing suspension of disbelief* was first used by the poet Coleridge to describe what happens when we read certain works of the imagination. Obviously, Ballard does not expect us to 'believe in' giants. Yet from the first

Commentary

we are presented with *the categorical fact* of the giant's existence. In order to read the story at all we must agree, temporarily, to 'suspend our disbelief', and it is a tribute to the quality of Ballard's imagination if we find it easy to do so. By what means does he encourage us to believe in the story?

When first discovered, the giant is lying two hundred yards out; by the end of the week, the body is jammed against a breakwater, not twenty yards from the shingle, and *all traces of magic* have disappeared. How does the narrator's description of the giant on the first day differ from the descriptions that follow later? What is the attitude of the crowd towards the initial sighting, and how does this attitude alter during the course of the week?

As a story, *The Drowned Giant* has an uneventful plot, and neither dialogue nor characters in the usual sense – the narrator is in fact the most developed 'character' in the story. He (or she) uses a noticeably wide and often technical vocabulary (what is s/he researching, do you think?), which is in itself an important part of the story's effect: it reads in places like an official report. However, the narrator's strong personal feelings concerning the *sequence of depredations* (amputations, graffiti and so on) are not in doubt – though they seem not to be shared by the other spectators, or by the contractors who soon appear on the scene. Re-read the paragraph beginning *I next visited* . . . on p. 120. Why *does* the giant's fate become important to the narrator?

What kind of story is *The Drowned Giant*? If it is purely imaginary, unrelated to the world we in fact know, then we might call it a fantasy – a kind of fairy-tale. But if the story of this *magnificent illusion* makes us think seriously about the world, then the fantasy has at least an element of fable: however unreal the story may seem, it has a serious purpose. How would you 'interpret' the story? What impression of human nature does it leave us with?

Ideas for writing

☐ What is *The Drowned Giant* about?
☐ Write two further short accounts of the giant. The first is spoken in a local pub, on the first evening, by one of the gang of youths (see p. 120) who had occupied the giant's head. The second is a report written three days later by one of the contractor's agents (see p. 122), informing his superiors of the commercial possibilities of the corpse. In each case, be sure to find a form of language appropriate for the character and the occasion.
☐ Try writing an unlikely story that nonetheless compels its readers to 'suspend their disbelief'.

Further reading

J G Ballard: *The Terminal Beach* (Gollancz, 1964; Penguin, 1966); *The Disaster Area* (Cape, 1967; Triad/Panther, 1979); *Myths of the Near Future* (Cape, 1982; Triad/Panther, 1984).

Commentary

The Handsomest Drowned Man in the World
Gabriel Garcia Marquez   Translated by Gregory Rabassa.

Gabriel Garcia Marquez is the one writer in this anthology who does not write in English. He is a Spanish-speaking South American, born in Colombia in 1928. His work first became known to English readers in 1970, when the extraordinary *One Hundred Years of Solitude* was published in an English translation. At that time, a novel by Marquez was quite unlike anything in English, though since then his influence has been considerable. In his novels and stories, the brute facts of Latin American history are interwoven with legend and myth, reminiscence and superstition. Comic and horrifying by turns, his books seem to be written out of the imagination of an entire people.

The Handsomest Drowned Man in the World is from *Leaf Storm* (1972).

Ideas for discussion

Garcia Marquez has remarked that a work of fiction is *reality represented through a kind of secret code, a kind of conundrum about the world . . . The same thing is true of dreams*. He has spoken dismissively of 'fantasy'; his claim is that everything in his books, however surprising, has some grounding in truth.

The point of similarity between *The Handsomest Drowned Man in the World* and *The Drowned Giant* is obvious enough. Somewhere behind both, I would imagine, lies the image of Lemuel Gulliver unconscious on the beach at Lilliput, in Swift's *Gulliver's Travels*. What makes the difference is the way in which each giant figure is treated. Ballard writes of *the city*, Garcia Marquez of *the village* – neither are named. How do these communities differ? Does that affect how the 'giant' is in each case received? Why do male and female villagers react differently to Esteban? (Spanish for 'Stephen'.)

In *The Drowned Giant*, the narrator is a clearly characterised figure, who is present in the story. Who *is* the narrator of *The Handsomest Drowned Man in the World* – where in the story does s/he belong? How would you describe the tone of the narrating voice – the attitudes and feelings conveyed in the way events are recorded?

It is worth comparing the last paragraph of *The Handsomest Drowned Man in the World* with the paragraph on p. 120 of *The Drowned Giant* noted previously. Garcia Marquez leaves us with the haunting image of a perfumed garden in the middle of an ocean. What, finally, has Esteban meant to the village?

Ideas for writing

☐ What interests you about this story?
☐ What differences are there between the villagers' treatment of Esteban, and the treatment received by the drowned giant in J G Ballard's story?
☐ Marquez calls this 'A tale for children' though *Leaf Storm* is hardly a children's book. Try writing a 'Tale for children' of this kind.

Further reading

Gabriel Garcia Marquez: *One Hundred Years of Solitude* (Picador, 1978); *Leaf Storm* (Picador, 1979); *Chronicle of a Death Foretold* (Picador, 1983).